CODE NAME PIGEON

CODE NAME PIGEON

Book 3: Elimination

A Novel

Girad Clacy

iUniverse, Inc.
New York Bloomington

Code Name Pigeon
Book 3: Elimination

iUniverse books may be ordered through booksellers or by contacting:

iUniverse
1663 Liberty Drive
Bloomington, IN 47403
www.iuniverse.com
1-800-Authors (1-800-288-4677)

ISBN: 978-1-4401-3074-8 (pbk)
ISBN: 978-1-4401-3075-5 (ebk)

Printed in the United States of America

iUniverse rev. date: 3/9/2009

For those who have served in areas that weren't friendly to anyone including beasts, this book is for you; also anyone who has ever had to deal with the dark side of humanity.

SPOT Agent Michael Pigeon

CHAPTER I

▼

Bill was thankful that Michael had not found out what he had been doing. Agent Hollister was still keeping an eye on Michael. He followed Michael to and from the airfield during the day and kept an eye on him during the evening hours. However, tonight, there was something nagging at the back of Agent Hollister's mind.

The feeling was something akin to impending doom. More than once, he had checked his rearview mirror for "tails." He didn't see any and therefore dismissed this feeling as an overactive imagination. Once Michael went to bed, Agent Hollister went to his own house and filed his report.

The next morning, however, Bill was in his office early when Agent Stallingsworth nearly kicked the door open. He barged right on into the office and slammed the door behind himself. He walked briskly over to Bill's desk and pounded his right fist onto the desktop hard.

"Just who in the hell do you think you are?!" Agent Stallingsworth yelled.

"I beg your pardon?" asked Bill in return, although he knew full well what the issue was that Stallingsworth was speaking about.

"Don't get stupid with me. You know exactly what I'm talking about!" He was now yelling much louder than just a few minutes ago.

"Well, for starters, I don't know what you're talking about. Secondly, maybe if you asked nicely instead of nearly ripping the doors off the hinges, you might get better answers. Now, what are you talking about that I am supposed to have been a party to?"

"I'm talking about sicking the goddamn FBI on me!" He pounded his right fist down again on the desktop.

"The FBI? What are you talking about?"

"I'm talking about using the disguise of the USA PATRIOT Act of 2001 to call an investigation on me and my doings."

"What makes you think I did it?"

"The statements that were made to the FBI agents that talked to me. Also, the fact that they have been following me around could have only come from orders issued by you."

"What statements?"

"You know what statements I'm talking about."

"I think you need a vacation, Agent Stallingsworth. In fact, I think that vacation should start right now," said Bill, reaching into his top left drawer of his desk to pull out some paperwork.

Bill started filling out the paperwork and in a few minutes, he signed the form. He handed the form over to Agent Stallingsworth and then closed the top left drawer of his desk. Agent Stallingsworth looked over the form and then stormed out of the office. He, once again, slammed the double-doors to Bill's office. As Agent Stallingsworth walked passed Bill's secretary, he pointed his left index finger at her. She looked at him surprised.

"Mark my words, Michael Pigeon and all his team members will die for this!"

"Why does he and his team have to die?" asked Bill's secretary.

"He overheard our conversation that we had a few weeks back."

"I see. Shall I alert our friends?"

"Not yet."

As Agent Stallingsworth left the outer office, he bumped into Agent Hollister. Agent Hollister smiled at Agent Stallingsworth and spoke to him in a nice tone of voice.

"Good morning Agent Stallingsworth, how are you today?"

Pointing his right index finger at Agent Hollister, Agent Stallingsworth narrowed his black eyes to almost twin slits.

"If you get in my way, I'll kill you!"

As he walked down the hallway towards the elevators, Agent Hollister stood there, perplexed. After a few seconds, he turned back around and started walking towards Bill's office. He mumbled to himself in the hallway as he walked into the outer office.

"And a pleasant good day to you too."

Bill's secretary looked up at him and then looked around the room. Since she didn't see anyone else, she just shrugged the whole thing off as case of hallucinations gone awry. She was about to talk to Agent Hollister when the phone rang. She picked up the receiver and put the call through to Bill.

In a few minutes, Bill opened the double-doors to his office and motioned for Agent Hollister to enter his office. Agent Hollister waited until the double-doors were shut and locked before he sat down in the chair that was to the left of Bill's desk.

"Who pissed Napalm into Agent Stallingsworth's breakfast this morning?" asked Agent Hollister.

"I did," replied Bill.

"Well, I kind of figured you did. How's the investigation going?"

"Not so well. I just got off the phone with the senior FBI agent in charge."

"What happened?"

"Agent Stallingsworth and his cronies slipped through our fingers."

"Oh no."

"Yes, and there is more to it than that."

"Like what?"

"Michael may now be in grave danger from Agent Stallingsworth as a target of retaliation. I want you to interfere with any plans Agent Stallingsworth may hatch to kill, injure, maim or harass Michael. Do you understand me?"

"I will do my best."

"By the way, where is Michael at right now?"

"He is at Jeannie's apartment in Littleton."

"Jeannie? You don't mean Jeannie Lyons, do you?"

"Yes. Is there something wrong with that?"

"Nothing's wrong, it's just that according to her personality profile test she took, she hates males."

"Oh, I see. Well she and Michael are getting along just fine."

"Okay. Please keep a closer eye on Michael from now on. Please call him on his cell phone and ask him to come in to my office."

"Sounds good."

Agent Hollister left Bill's office and headed for the parking garage. Once he was clear of the parking garage, he called Michael's cell phone. The phone didn't ring, but went straight into the voicemail. Hollister waited for the tone to sound and then left Michael a message to come into the office. Hollister waited for a second or two before putting the cell phone he was using back down into the ashtray. As Agent Hollister headed into Littleton, that strange sense of danger being very close reared its head.

Meanwhile, Michael had just finished having sex with Jeannie, when he decided that he was hungry. Trying not to disturb Jeannie as he slipped out of bed and started putting his clothes on, she turned over to face him. She opened her left eye and watched him get dressed.

"Leaving so soon?" she asked Michael.

"No. I'm hungry and I thought that since there isn't much here for breakfast, that I would go to the store and get the fixings for breakfast," replied Michael.

"Sounds good, hurry back," she said as she turned back over and went back to sleep.

Michael put on the rest of his clothes and left her apartment. He was careful to set the self-locking lock to lock when the door was closed. He also knew that when he returned, he would hopefully find her awake and she would let him inside the apartment.

Michael arrived at his car and checked it over for booby traps and explosive devices. Finding none, he opened the driver's side door and stepped into the car. He started the car up and drove to the store. Along the way, he passed Agent Hollister, although he didn't know it at the time.

Agent Hollister was wearing a disguise and Michael wasn't really expecting anyone to be following him around. He made a note of the time that Michael had departed the apartment complex. After this, Agent Hollister started up his own car and drove to the store where he parked in the parking lot just a few cars down from Michael's.

While Michael was inside the store, Agent Stallingsworth was putting the final touches on his plan to systematically eliminate

Michael's entire team. As he finished off the call to his terrorist friends, he decided to start the killings off by eliminating Bill's friend, Agent Hollister, first.

Agent Stallingsworth put his cell phone back into his left jacket pocket. Next, he unholstered his weapon and checked the semi-automatic to make sure that it was fully loaded. As he put the gun back into his holster, he reached under the seat of his car and withdrew a small, brown satchel.

He opened up the satchel and started searching through the contents with his right hand until he found what he was looking for; the silencer for his gun. He took the silencer out of the satchel and carefully screwed it onto the barrel of his Smith and Wesson® Model 4506-1, .45-caliber pistol. He finally put the pistol back into the holster and started up his car. He drove off into the rising sun to a destination only he knew.

Michael had purchased the breakfast items and had put them into the trunk of his car, when he decided to turn on his cell phone. As the cell phone powered up, it signaled to Michael that there was a pending message. Michael opened the face of the cell phone and looked at the display screen. The message symbol was in the middle of the upper part of the screen. He pushed the "*" key on the keypad and accessed his voicemail. Bill had labeled the message as "urgent". Michael listened to the message and deleted it thereafter. He then turned the cell phone back off and drove back to Jeannie's place.

After Michael had fixed them breakfast, she cleaned up the dishes. They then went into her living room and sat down on the couch. As they both read different sections of the morning paper, Michael put up the section of the paper he was reading and looked at his watch. He stood up, grabbing his light jacket and heading for the door.

"Going somewhere?" asked Jeannie.

"Yes, I'm going to the airfield for my daily flight time and then from there I will have to stop by the office. Bill left me a message and he seemed pretty insistent that I come by his office today," replied Michael.

"Are we going to get together tonight?"

"I think that is possible. However, I do have to do laundry and perform other errands today."

"I understand. Will you call me?"

"Yes, I will call you."

Michael left Jeannie's apartment and she locked the door behind him. As she set about cleaning up the rest of the apartment, she had no idea that Agent Stallingsworth was waiting for the right moment to kill her. He was a man with nothing but doing evil on his mind. As he sat in his car, he looked down into his lap as Michael drove by him headed towards the airfield. Agent Hollister followed him a short time later.

Again Agent Stallingsworth looked down into his lap. In his lap was his pistol with the silencer attached. Agent Stallingsworth waited until Hollister was gone and then turned over the engine of his own car. Stallingsworth followed Hollister at a very, very discreet distance.

Agent Hollister parked his car at the end of the perimeter fence and pulled out his binoculars. Using the binoculars, he could keep an eye on Michael and Michael wouldn't know he was being watched. Agent Hollister watched as Michael took off in the twin-engine aircraft and then returned a short while later.

He then stepped into the helicopter for about two hours. At the end of this, Agent Hollister decided that since it was about lunchtime, he would go to the sub sandwich shop at the other end of the airfield for lunch. Once he had returned from lunch, Agent Stallingsworth was carefully preparing to kill Agent Hollister and Jeannie when the chance arose.

Shortly after lunch, Michael went to his apartment and started his laundry. After the laundry went into the dryer, he went downtown to see what Bill wanted to talk to him about. Agent Hollister went to the building, but stayed inside his car outside the entrance/exit point of the parking garage. Michael was unaware that he was even being followed.

Agent Hollister had no idea that Agent Stallingsworth had gone to Agent Hollister's home. Agent Stallingsworth had parked a few houses down the street and took refuge inside the bushes. Agent Stallingsworth had decided to use a blitz style of attack against Agent Hollister.

Agent Stallingsworth carefully looked over his plans. He wanted to leave nothing to chance. He had on rubber gloves and was carrying a small, black bag. Inside the black bag were the tools that he would need to complete tonight's killing. He checked the silencer once more and then stretched out into the bushes to await Agent Hollister's arrival.

Meanwhile, Michael was finally able to get into Bill's office. Bill's secretary had told Michael that he was on a conference call with the Secretary of State. As he entered the office, Bill shut and locked the double-doors. Bill pointed to a chair that was to the right of his desk. Michael sat down in it and Bill looked at him straight into his eyes.

"Michael, I have some rather distressing news," Bill started off saying.

"Oh, what's that?" Michael almost knew what the answer was.

"Despite our best efforts, Agent Stallingsworth slipped through our fingers. I have a copy of the FBI report if you want to review it. Michael, I am so sorry."

Michael narrowed his eyes a little bit before returning his eyebrows to their normal position. He took in a deep breath. He then let it out slowly. For Michael, this news was not unexpected, but it did throw him for a loop. Bill set down in front of Michael on the desktop, a copy of the FBI report.

"Its okay, Bill I actually kind of expected this to happen. It's just that, he's getting away with the murder of at least three SPOT agents and I'm sure that he's behind the attempts on my life."

"Michael, I know he is, too; however, he's just a little slicker than we thought he might be. Don't give up trying to bring him to justice, just yet," replied Bill.

At hearing these words, Michael started to smile. Those words, Michael realized, where the polite way of saying, *"Stay on Agent Stallingsworth's tail. He will trip one day, you need to be ready to catch him."*

"I understand, Bill. You did what you could based upon what I reported to you."

"If you want to talk about it after reading the FBI report, all you have to do is call."

"I'll take this home for some light reading," said Michael as he walked out the door.

On the way out of Bill's office, Michael shot an evil looking sideways glance at Bill's secretary. He then stood right in front of her and glared at her for just a few seconds. He then leaned down to her level and whispered in her right ear.

"How much blood money have you been paid to become a traitor to your own kind?"

She jumped back a little as Michael walked out of the office. She waited until he was down the hallway before calling Agent Stallingsworth's restricted cell phone number.

"Yes, what can I do for you?" asked Agent Stallingsworth.

"Michael Pigeon knows what is going on, Harry," she said.

"Then Michael Pigeon will have to die for that knowledge."

"I didn't like him getting into my face and saying what he did just before he walked out of here this evening."

"I'll be taking care of him and his friends."

"Make it soon, good-bye."

She hung up the phone and went back to typing and filing. For her, to know that Michael knew she was involved was disquieting to say the least. Meanwhile, Michael had departed the parking garage and picked up his discreet "tail." Agent Hollister followed Michael back to his apartment.

Once Michael was back at his apartment, he went back down to the laundry room and found that the clothes were dry. He put them into the laundry basket that he had taken down there earlier and then returned to his apartment where he started to sort and fold his clean clothes.

After he had finished that, he looked at his watch. It was 1715 hours and he had promised to call Jeannie when he was finished with Bill. He walked into the kitchen, picked up the receiver and dialed her number. The phone rang a few times before she answered.

"Hello?" she said.

"Hello there, Jeannie. I just finished off with both my laundry and that appointment with Bill."

"Good to hear from you Michael. Are we going on a mission?"

"No, no mission this time. The appointment was for other reasons."

"Are you going to come over?"

"Yes, I am, I thought we could have a little dinner and practice our foreign language skills."

"Sounds great. I'll start cooking the pasta right now."

"I'll see you in just a little while," said Michael, as he hung up the phone.

Agent Hollister smiled as he watched Michael leave his apartment and start heading towards Jeannie's apartment in Littleton. Agent Hollister followed him to Jeannie's apartment and watched him go inside. Once he was inside, Agent Hollister started to drive back to his house.

During the drive to his house, that sense of impending doom came back to him. The sense was almost stabbing him in the back of his mind that something bad was going to happen. Agent Hollister ignored this warning sign, shrugging it off to too much stress of having to keep tabs on Michael and making sure that he didn't get into any trouble.

As Agent Hollister pulled into his driveway, that sense of impending doom was at the point of screaming inside his mind. He parked his car and turned off the engine. He stepped out of his car and carefully looked around his surroundings, looking for anything out of the ordinary. He looked at everything and found nothing out of the ordinary. He turned his back to the bushes and closed the driver's side, car door, locking it up for the night. The porch light was on, but the dim light bulb wasn't giving off enough light to deter Agent Stallingsworth from carrying out his gruesome plan for Agent Hollister.

CHAPTER 2

▼

Agent Hollister was standing on his front porch, putting the key into the deadbolt lock on his front door, when Agent Stallingsworth attacked him. Agent Stallingsworth had stayed hidden in the shadows and took only three giant steps to be within a short distance-shooting scenario. Agent Hollister heard the bushes rattling and by the time he looked back towards them, Agent Stallingsworth appeared at the corner of his house. Agent Stallingsworth took aim and put all nine rounds into Agent Hollister. Agent Stallingsworth picked up the black bag that he had brought with him and went to work.

Calmly, Agent Stallingsworth waited at the side of the house in the shadows for Agent Hollister to finally slump down the front door. Agent Hollister's dead body came to a stop, in a lumpy heap, on the front porch. Agent Stallingsworth walked out of the shadows and reloaded his pistol after he had set down the black bag that he had been carrying in his left hand.

A faint wisp of smoke emanated from the barrel as Agent Stallingsworth took the silencer off the pistol. He reholstered the weapon and put the silencer into his black jacket pocket. As he approached Agent Hollister's dead body, he glanced once up to the porch light.

Reaching into the black bag that he was carrying in his left hand, he grabbed a short piece of wood. He used this piece of wood to break the light cover hard enough to break the light bulb off. Now, as he looked around the neighborhood for signs that this action had been heard, he looked down at Agent Hollister's body.

Seeing that no lights had come on in the adjacent houses with the breaking of the glass, he put the short piece of wood back into the bag. He reached into the bag once more and removed the night vision goggles. He turned them on and started dragging the dead body, with his right arm, over to the opposite side of the yard. Agent Stallingsworth dragged the body over to near the bushes behind the tree that was in the front yard. There, Stallingsworth smiled at his handy work.

Setting the bag down on the ground, he removed a pair of pliers. He started fishing around inside each of the bullet holes that he had made and found the bullet. In some cases the bullet had severely fragmented, but all in all, Stallingsworth managed to collect all the bullets from Hollister's body. After Stallingsworth had collected all the bullets, he put them and their fragments into a plastic bag that had been labeled, "AGENT HOLLISTER."

Next, Stallingsworth put the plastic bag back into the black bag he had carried with him. He reached back into the bag and withdrew a small medical kit containing sutures. Carefully, he sewed up the bullet holes in the body and smiled at himself for his ingenuity. Once this was completed, Stallingsworth carefully checked around the neighborhood and went over to where he had been standing earlier. He switched from normal night vision to night vision with infrared.

He waited a minute or two so that the night vision goggles could recalibrate themselves. Once this had been completed, Stallingsworth looked around on the ground. He reached into his bag and pulled out another plastic bag and started picking up all the spent shell casings. After the last spent shell casing had been picked up, he put the plastic bag back into the bag he was carrying and walked towards his car. Next, Stallingsworth completed the task by cleaning up the blood that had been left behind by the body. Looking around carefully with the goggles on their maximum magnification, he used a fallen tree branch that was next to the sidewalk, to obliterate his footprints.

When he was certain that no one had seen him, he took off the goggles and put them into the bag as well. Next, he opened the driver's side door and stepped into his vehicle. Stallingsworth started the engine, turned on the lights and drove off into the night. He was heading towards his secret lair.

Stallingsworth arrived at his lair about an hour later. The place was a deserted warehouse that had, at one time, been a small welding shop. The equipment was still there, but no one checked on the place. It was located outside a small suburb of Denver called Federal Heights. He parked the car, opened the side door to the warehouse and closed it behind him.

Moments later, Stallingsworth, dressed in different clothes than the ones he had used to kill Hollister with, opened the passenger's side back door and removed the black bag from the back seat. He reentered the warehouse and put the black bag with all the other clothes on top of an old, steel-welding table. He then put on some welding goggles.

Stallingsworth started up the torch unit that had been leftover from the welding shop days and completely burned all the evidence to nothing. He even went so far as to make sure that there wasn't even any ash left by keeping the torch in close contact with the items until nothing remained. After he shut off the torch unit, he removed his goggles and looked around on the floor for any signs that he had not completely destroyed the evidence.

Since nothing remained, he decided to celebrate a little with some alcohol that he had brought along earlier that day to the warehouse. He had just sat down on the couch that had been leftover from the warehouse days when he closed his eyes and the drink that he had made slipped from his right hand and crashed onto the floor. Just behind him, in a rusty looking old locker, were more of these bags. Each bag had all the SPOT agent's names on them.

Meanwhile, Bill had come into work. His secretary handed him a stack of messages and he started to look them over. He noticed as he entered his office and shut the doors behind himself, that Agent Hollister had not reported since last night on Michael's whereabouts. He looked down at his watch and decided to give Agent Hollister until 1000 hours before calling him to find out what was going on with him and Michael. Bill sat down at his desk and started returning phone calls and busied himself with the morning rush.

When 1000 hours came and went with still no word, Bill called Michael and asked him to stop by Agent Hollister's house in the Cherry Creek area of Denver to see if he was all right. Bill had made up the excuse that Agent Hollister hadn't been feeling well the last few days. Bill knew that Agent Hollister was perfectly fine, however he needed to tell Michael something so that Michael would go and check on him without being suspicious. Since Michael had not turned on his cell phone yet, Bill had to leave the message in the cell phone's voicemail box.

Meanwhile, Michael was again fixing breakfast for himself and Jeannie. Michael was beginning to enjoy the time that she and him had been spending together. Michael felt as though there was something different about her than the other women on the SPOT team. He had the distinct impression from some of her references to other males she had dated, that she didn't like males in general.

Michael came to the conclusion that Jeannie liked him because everything they did was on a professional level and not the social level. Although, Michael was concerned that they were having sex on a fairly regular basis since they started seeing each other following the executive security mission. To Michael, having sex was anything but a professional thing.

After a shower, Michael turned on his cell phone. The message symbol showed up in the menu display once again. He dialed into his voicemail and heard Bill's message. After hearing the message, he deleted it and hung up the phone. Clipping the cell phone to the right front pocket of his jeans, he turned around and smiled at Jeannie.

"I received another phone call from Bill. He wants me to check up on Agent Hollister," said Michael.

"Okay, not a problem. Harold called here yesterday while you were at the grocery store and asked if you would be interested in sparring with him later on tonight," said Jeannie.

"Would you mind if I went and participated in this sparring event with him?" asked Michael.

"No, go ahead. Besides, we have spent a lot of time together recently. I need some time to clean up the place and you need some time for yourself; call me when you get done?"

"Sure thing. Goodbye," said Michael as he headed out the door.

As Michael completed his vehicle inspection, he looked around the parking lot. Making sure that no one was watching him, he unholstered his .44 magnum revolver and checked the cylinder to make sure it was full. After checking the cylinder, he closed the cylinder back up and reholstered his weapon. He stepped into his car and drove off towards the address that Bill had given him for Agent Hollister. Michael drove on through the rest of the late morning and into the early afternoon before arriving at Agent Hollister's house.

Suddenly, Michael's Sixth sense told him something was very wrong. Remembering that his executive security instructor had told him in class to listen to this "early warning system," he slowed his car down and parked a few houses up from Hollister's house. He stepped out of his car and started walking towards Hollister's house.

He walked up the driveway and saw that Hollister's car was still there. He then checked the car doors and found them locked. It wasn't until he arrived at the front door that he knew something was wrong.

Michael went to knock on the front door, but stopped himself as he looked down the front door. The key was still inserted into the deadbolt part of the lock. Michael began to immediately assess the situation at hand. He unsnapped the retaining strap on his shoulder holster and slightly lifted the revolver out of the holster. This was a trick that he had learned while in executive security school to make it easier and faster to draw the weapon.

Reaching into the left back pocket of his pants, Michael withdrew a clean handkerchief and tried the key to see if it was unlocked or locked. The key had been turned, from Michael's point of view, about one quarter of the way to the left. When Michael completed the cycle, he tried the doorknob. Turning it slowly he opened the door. Once the door was fully opened, he put the handkerchief back up and drew the weapon.

Michael completed what he had been taught as "room clearing" in a law enforcement class that he had taken, in just a few minutes. There were no signs of a struggle nor were there any signs of Agent Hollister. Michael walked back out the door and looked around the front yard. There, faintly visible in the grass, were a pair of shoes.

The shoes were sticking out just enough to be found, but not found easily. Michael ran out there to find that those shoes belonged to Agent Hollister. Rolling over Agent Hollister's body, Michael found the gruesome details of his demise. Michael gently rolled Agent Hollister's body back over to the side position and stood up. As he stood up, he grabbed his cell phone and called Bill's office.

"Good afternoon, Michael, what can I do for you?" asked Bill jubilantly.

Michael thought for about a minute how he was going to tell Bill that Hollister was dead. He decided that a direct approach was best.

"A pleasant good afternoon to you too, Bill. I have accomplished that mission that you asked me to perform today."

"Great, what was the outcome of this mission?"

"He is dead."

"Don't move. I'm sending over the police and our own personnel. Do not leave the area until I get there."

"Yes, sir."

Within minutes, the police department showed up with their mobile crime laboratory. They completed up their side of the investigation and left just as the special forensics team from the SPOT unit arrived. They took copies of the police department's reports and interviews with the neighbors and Michael. They noticed right away Michael had not said much of anything. Bill arrived just a few minutes later and found Michael sitting on the front bumper of his car. Bill walked over to Michael and started asking him questions.

"I'm glad you called me. Now, tell me what you didn't tell the police," said Bill.

"I found Agent Hollister over there by the tree, opposite the front door. The key was still in the deadbolt lock of the front door at about a one quarter turn to the left," Michael started out saying.

"Meaning that the door was locked or unlocked?"

"I'm going to surmise that he was unlocking the door when the attack happened."

"Go on."

"I saw no signs of forced entry, no struggle took place."

"What do you think happened?"

"I suppose that since this is not the nicest neighborhood around, it could have been a drive-by shooting. However, I don't think so."

"What makes you think this wasn't a drive-by?"

"Agent Hollister's weapon was still holstered. Either it happened very, very quickly and extremely quietly or else he knew his attacker."

"What evidence do you have to support this theory?"

"For one, nobody heard any gunshots at all. That tells me that whomever did this was using a silencer. Highly illegal, unless you have the proper license from the federal government for it, from what I remember in our SPOT agent classes."

"True, silencers are highly regulated. What other evidence do you have to support your theory?"

"Since Hollister didn't draw his weapon out to defend himself, he must have known who his attacker was. Or he never heard them coming, which is possible, but not likely."

"Why?"

"Agent Hollister taught all of us at the SPOT agent school about personal security in lots of areas. I just can't imagine him letting someone get that close without firing off a round or yelling at them or something that would have received a lot of attention to his house."

Bill thought about that statement for a few seconds and knew Michael was right.

"You're right about that. Anything else that you think of, don't hesitate to call me. Even if it is the slightest minute detail, call me."

"Yes, sir."

"Dismissed and stay on your toes."

As Bill walked away, Michael was standing perplexed by this statement. Michael started wondering what Bill was trying to tell him without telling him. Michael drove away from the grisly scene and went back to his apartment. He changed clothes to his workout attire and drove to the office.

Michael parked his car and took the holster out of the towel that he had wrapped it up inside and traded the .44 magnum for his Taurus® PT-100, SSPL. He asked for all five magazines and loaded them all up with silvertip hollow points, before going to the sparring match.

The sparring match was with SPOT Agent Glen Armstrong. He was Korean by birth and had been working out since he was about 17 years old. His body was well trimmed and well balanced with endurance in his muscle structure rather than brute strength. Michael started stretching out first, as did Glen. After they were through stretching, they worked on the basic moves before putting on the safety gear.

After sparring with each other with and without the safety gear on, Glen called it a night and so did Michael. They both showered and Glen left shortly before Michael did. Michael waited until he was out of the parking garage to call Jeannie. She had just finished cleaning up the whole apartment and said she was tired. Michael said he understood that and he went home.

Meanwhile, Agent Stallingsworth was waiting for Agent Armstrong. Glen arrived home. Waiting just inside the outer doorway to the house, in the dark, was Agent Stallingsworth. Agent Stallingsworth had already forced access to his house and killed everyone in there. Again, he cleaned up all the evidence that would link him to such a crime. As Glen walked towards his house, Agent Stallingsworth attacked him with great speed.

Agent Stallingsworth shot Agent Armstrong to death. Once again he removed the evidence and destroyed it back at the warehouse. Stallingsworth was feeling pretty proud of himself. Each time he was getting better and better at the killing and making sure he took the evidence with him. Stallingsworth replenished the black bag's supplies for, in a few nights, he was going to kill the next SPOT agent that had any contact with Michael Pigeon. SPOT Agent Jeannie Lyons was next on the list.

Agent Stallingsworth was smiling gleefully as he poured himself another drink. Agent Armstrong's body wasn't discovered until the next morning. It was the newspaper delivery person delivering the morning paper that found the grisly scene of death. Again there were no witnesses; nobody heard anything nor did they see anything.

The police were baffled and Bill was informed that there was another SPOT agent found dead at his house along with his entire family. Agent Armstrong was married with three children. All of them including his newborn son were shot to death.

Bill looked over the police report on Agent Armstrong's death and read the coroner's report on Agent Hollister. There were haunting similarities to the killings. Bill suddenly realized that another SPOT agent or someone with similar abilities killed those agents. Bill had a sinking feeling in his stomach that the person responsible was possibly SPOT Agent Harry Stallingsworth. Bill decided to call Michael. As Bill looked down at the clock on his desktop, he realized it might already be too late to stop the killings.

CHAPTER 3

▼

Bill was rereading both the police reports and the coroner's reports. He couldn't fathom the mentality of the monster it took to kill a seven-month-old baby in its crib with a firearm. As he set the reports back down on his desktop, one thing was clear to him. The coroner's reports on the dead bodies all indicated that they had been probably shot to death with the same type of firearm. Bill asked the coroner to determine the type of firearm. The coroner stated in all of the post mortems that determining what kind of firearm was used would be difficult.

Since, the coroner stated in his reports, that the killer cleaned up the evidence very thoroughly, by stitching the bullet holes shut, and taking the bullets and their fragments with them, he couldn't tell Bill the answer to that question. Bill called the coroner back this morning to ask some more questions.

"Yes, Mr. Yancy, what can I do for you?" asked the coroner, whom he had been dealing with the past few days.

"Even though there are no bullets, only fragments too small to be of any use to anyone for a ballistics analysis, can you tell me by measuring the bullet entry wounds, even though I know they were stitched shut, what the estimated type of the firearm might be?"

Bill was hoping that maybe the coroner could come up with a measurement. Bill would then take this measurement and cross-reference this with the SPOT agent files. Maybe, just maybe, the killer might have left behind something despite his handiwork.

"Alright, Mr. Yancy, I will measure one of those bullet holes. Can I call you back?"

"I'll wait on the line, thank you," replied Bill.

"I'll be right back."

The phone receiver was set down and in a few minutes, the coroner returned to the phone. He picked up the receiver and started talking to Bill once again.

"The bullet holes measure .453 inches."

"Thank you very much, you have been a great help."

Bill hung up the phone. He knew from the coroner's tentative examination of the bullet wounds that the measurement was from one of many .45 caliber cartridges which included the .45AUTORIM, .45 ACP, .45 GAP rounds or possibly, a .45 Winchester® Magnum round.

Now, Bill's next step was to order a search of the files of all the SPOT agents assigned to the Denver office. Bill wanted a list compiled of all SPOT agents that have a .45 caliber pistol assigned to them. Bill picked up his phone and called the main Internal Affairs office for the SPOT corps in Miami, Florida.

"Good afternoon, Internal Affairs for the Special Projects and Operations Taskforce corps. This is Linda, how may I help you?" she said, pleasantly.

"This is Bill Yancy, code clearance Red. I need to request for procedure 004."

"Yes, sir. I will submit this request. Expect an answer in 24 to 48 hours."

"Yes, ma'am and thank you."

After Bill hung up the phone, he looked down at the newspaper that was on his desk. Thankfully, as of yet, no reports of the killings had reached the news. Bill suddenly realized that he would have to keep these killings suppressed so that the general public wouldn't panic. Picking up the phone again, he called the Secretary of State on her cell phone.

"Yes, Bill, what can I do for you?" she asked as she looked across the table at Agent Stallingsworth.

"I think I have a possible renegade SPOT agent. I need to request for a suppression of the 1st Amendment here in Denver before the word gets out," said Bill as calmly as he could.

There was silence at the other end before Lillian answered.

"Okay, I will call the National Security Agency and talk to the appropriate people."

"Thank you very much; goodbye."

"Goodbye."

Bill hung up the phone and sat back in his chair. He spun the chair around to face out the window and looked into the distant mountains. After about an hour, the phone rang. He spun back around in his chair and picked up the receiver.

"Hello?" said Bill.

"Bill, I explained the position to the appropriate people at the National Security Agency and they agreed with you. Your court order suppressing the 1st Amendment will be delivered to you by the close of business today."

"I thank you for your tact and diplomacy during this time."

"You're welcome and goodbye."

Bill hung up the phone as Lillian put the receiver back down into the cradle. She looked up at Agent Stallingsworth who was smiling very large. She looked at him for just a minute and then stood up to tower over him.

"Are you sure that gun is untraceable?"

"Quite sure. In fact, I reported it as being stolen, missing or damaged during *Operation Blue Ball* eight years ago. I even filed the appropriate paperwork with Bill. I believe it is a Form 1464 for reporting 'Lost, Stolen or Damaged Government Issued Equipment or Property.'"

"And there is no chance of any of this getting back to me or me being connected with it somehow?" she asked nervously.

"Not a chance. I destroy all the evidence and no one even knows that I'm there. I take the bullets and their associated large fragments with me and I'm careful to stitch up the bullet holes afterwards."

"Okay, well you had better get back to Denver before Bill gets suspicious."

"On my way."

Agent Stallingsworth stepped out of Lillian's office and headed towards the airport. Once he was at his departure gate, he started smiling once again. His plane took off and Bill had no idea what was going on with these killings. All Bill had were suspicions and nothing more to go on. Although this frustrated Bill, he made the best of the frustration. Bill pressed his back up against his office chair and dialed Michael's number. Michael answered almost immediately.

"Hello, Bill, good to hear from you. What's going on?" asked Michael.

"Could you come into the office right away? I need you to deliver something to someone."

"Okay, I'm just leaving the airfield. I can be there in about 30 minutes. Is that soon enough?"

"Fine; goodbye."

Bill hung up the phone just as there came a knock on his office door. Bill cleared off his desk and looked at the double-doors. He readjusted his tie and then placed both hands on his desktop.

"Enter," said Bill loudly.

The door opened and a young man, dressed in business casual clothing, entered his office. After Bill's secretary shut the door behind the young man, Bill stood up and looked at the person. The person was holding a large, manila colored envelope, which he presented to Bill. The man, without saying a word, then turned around and walked out of the office.

Bill waited until the office doors had shut, before he opened up the envelope. He removed the envelope's contents and made sure that a local judge had signed the paperwork that he held in his hands. The Honorable Judge Joe Aberdeen of the Second Federal District court that held jurisdiction over the city of Denver, Colorado, signed the paperwork.

Bill looked up again as there was another knock on the door. He put the paperwork behind his back in his right hand and looked at the door. He then realized that it might have already been 30 minutes since he last talked to Michael. Looking up at the clock above the door, the clock indicated that 45 minutes had elapsed since he had talked to Michael. Bill smiled and stood up stiffly.

"Enter," said Bill, loudly, once again.

Michael entered the room and could immediately feel the awful tension in the room. Michael unconsciously stiffened up as well. Bill removed his right hand from behind his back and gave Michael the paperwork.

Michael looked the paperwork over and read the caption at the top of the first page. SUPPRESSION OF THE 1ST AMENDMENT AS AUTHORIZED BY THE NATIONAL SECURITY AGENCY..."
Michael looked up at Bill for some kind of recognition sign; he found almost none. In fact, from Michael's point of view, there was almost no emotion whatsoever on Bill's face.

"What is my mission?" asked Michael mechanically.

"You are to take that paperwork to the local newspaper and serve that court order on the editor."

"Yes, sir."

Michael walked out the door and went straight to the local newspaper. Michael walked into the building and spoke with the editor directly. Michael dropped the court order on the editor's desk. The editor read the court order and then looked up at Michael in stunned silence before speaking.

"Is this a joke? I mean, suppressing the 1st Amendment right?" asked the editor.

"Those are the orders from the National Security Agency. That court order you have in front of you has been signed by a federal judge that has jurisdiction over the State of Colorado."

"I understand, sir. This court order will be complied with; goodbye."

"Goodbye, sir."

Michael left the editor's office. The editor was looking down at the evening's edition. He noticed that the murders of those two agents and of the one agent's family was on page 78. Now, he had to pull the story and replace it with something else.

He called the reporter that had brought him the story, into his office and served her with a copy of the court order. They were both flabbergasted that the U.S. government would do such a thing. Michael returned to his apartment and called Bill.

"Mission accomplished at 1502 hours," said Michael without feeling.

"Well done. Please await my further instructions."

"Yes, sir."

Michael hung up the phone that he was using in the kitchen and picked up his cell phone. He stood by the sliding glass door that went out to the small balcony that he had at his apartment. He was calling Jeannie and not aware that just the other side of the curtains, was Agent Stallingsworth. Agent Stallingsworth was systematically eliminating the SPOT team.

Now, happily for him, he was down to four people. As Agent Stallingsworth put the silencer back on his pistol, he put on a pair of headphones. These headphones were connected to a tape recorder. From the tape recorder, the plug-in microphone was actually a small dish.

The small dish was a laser transmitter and Agent Stallingsworth was about to eavesdrop on the conversation that Michael was going to have with Agent Lyons. He smiled at the clarity of the transmission from so far away.

"Michael, good to hear from you. What do you have planned tonight?" asked Agent Lyons.

"I thought we could get together for some more foreign language conversations and I'll cook dinner," said Michael.

"That sounds great. When can I expect you over?"

"In about an hour."

"Great, see you then."

"Oh, by the way, have some of the red wine that I brought over a couple of days ago ready. It will go good with dinner."

"You're on, see you soon."

"Goodbye," Michael said, hanging up his cell phone.

Agent Stallingsworth moved into action. He looked at his watch and then at his map. He noted that he was less than an hour away from where Agent Lyons lived. Agent Stallingsworth started the car and drove over to her apartment complex in Littleton.

He put on his black clothing so that he would be hard to see in the dimly lighted hallways of the complex. He carried with him his bag and when he approached the apartment that Agent Lyons lived in, he pulled out his pistol. He rang the doorbell and she happily opened the door.

Agent Stallingsworth tossed the black bag at her to catch her off guard. Next, as she stood there in the doorway opening of her apartment, Stallingsworth calmly shot her in the head. She fell backwards onto the floor, dropping the bag. He quickly entered the apartment and put two more bullets into her head. The other rounds went into her body.

As she lay there on the floor, she was drenched in her own blood. Calmly, Stallingsworth took out the equipment from the bag that was lying on the floor and did his handy work. He looked down at his watch as it started beeping at him. This was a prearranged signal to give him plenty of time to leave the area before Michael arrived.

With the last of the evidence in the bag, he looked around her apartment and smiled. He walked out the door and left it slightly open. He wanted Michael to find it that way as a mark that he had been there. He also wanted to show Michael that he was still too inexperienced to ever find out who was doing these killings.

Stallingsworth stepped out the bottom door to the apartment complex and walked over to his car that he had parked a short distance away. He opened the driver's side, car door and tossed the bag into the front seat. He then stepped into the car, started the engine and drove off just as Michael was entering the complex from the opposite side. Michael never saw Agent Stallingsworth leaving and, again, no one would ever recall seeing him around the apartment complex.

Michael, who had stopped by the grocery store before going to Agent Lyons' apartment, parked his car in the "Visitor's" spot right next to her car. He stepped out of his car and grabbed the bag of groceries. He went to press the call button for her apartment, but a young couple came out the door instead. Michael smiled at them and walked up the short flight of stairs to the landing where her apartment was located. He walked down the hallway and came around the corner. He saw the slightly opened door.

Quickly he set down the groceries and pulled out his weapon. Carefully he scanned from right to left and up and down in the entryway to check for anyone standing there. Finding no one, he took two steps forward and smelled it.

There, hanging heavily in the air was the smell of burnt gunpowder. It was more commonly referred to as Cordite. Cautiously, he kept his pistol at the ready and kicked open the partially open door to Jeannie's apartment. As he moved into the doorway, his foot hit something. He looked down and saw her dead body lying there on the floor completely covered in her own blood.

Michael put his pistol up and checked her vital signs. Finding that she had multiple gunshot wounds to both the head and torso, he felt for a pulse and didn't find one. He then reached across her body and dialed 911 from the cordless phone that was lying on the floor next to her. After that, he called Bill's private number at his home.

"Yes, Michael, what is it?" asked Bill.

"Agent Lyons is dead. I found her body about five minutes ago," said Michael, trying to hold back the tears.

"I understand. I'll send someone over right away. Remember, don't talk too much to the police."

"Yes, sir."

Both the police and the ambulance showed up a short while later. The ambulance crew tried to revive her without success. They took her away to the morgue for a coroner's examination. Michael was interviewed by the police and released when the special crime laboratory showed up to check things out. As Michael was leaving her apartment, he looked down at the now spoiled groceries and picked them up.

He walked down to the dumpster and threw the bags into the dumpster. He was heading towards his car, when he recognized Agent Dill coming towards him. Agent Dill stopped a short distance back from Michael's car and showed Michael his badge.

"It's okay, Agent Dill, I'm all right," said Michael with a heavy heart.

"Now that you know who I am, can I ask you some questions?" said Agent Dill, pulling out a small note pad from his left jacket pocket and pulling out the pen that was inside the spiral backing of the note pad.

"Sure, go ahead," said Michael.

"Do you own a .45 caliber pistol?"

"Yes, a Glock® Model 21."

"Do you own, or have you had issued to you, a silencer?"

"Yes, I have a silencer issued to me from one of the shooting schools that I attended."

"I see," remarked Agent Dill, as he was writing down some notes on a small note pad.

"Is there anything else I can do for you?"

"When was the last time you fired your Glock?"

"Three weeks ago at the firing range."

"Have you checked out your Glock in the last five days?"

"No."

"Have you ever used the silencer?"

"No. In fact, I am supposed to have special instruction on how to use the silencer from the armorer. That lesson is supposed to take place next week."

"Okay. What weapon are you carrying now?"

"My Taurus® Model PT-100, SSPL."

"Is that the .40 Smith and Wesson Taurus?"

"Yes, it is."

"Okay. To let you know, you are not a suspect in these killings. Do you wish to discuss the killings with me at some point tomorrow?"

"Yes, I would like to know who it is that is systematically eliminating my team and has made an attempt on my life a couple of times."

"I'll see you tomorrow morning at Bill's office around 0945 hours."

"I'll be there."

Agent Dill put up the note pad and pen as he walked off to get into his car. He drove off as Michael went home. He thoroughly checked over his apartment to make sure that no one was waiting to kill him as well. Once he was inside, he locked the door and set his alarm clock. After this was done, he pulled the weapon out of its shoulder holster carry spot and placed it on the nightstand.

He started to close his eyes, but instead, cried himself to sleep. Michael was tough, but even that grisly scene was too much for him. It seemed like he had just closed his eyes, when the alarm clock went off.

CHAPTER 4

▼

The next morning, Bill's office was bustling with lots of people. Everyone in the office was terrified and now everyone, by Bill's orders, were arming themselves, including his secretary. Agent Dill had brought along six other agents from the Miami, Florida office to assist with the investigation into the killings. As information was gathered, Dill would review it and make copies of everything.

Once the copies were made, he would put all the information into the file folder. The file folder was labeled with a special code so that anyone looking for the file would find it most difficult to find the file. After the last of the information from this morning was compiled, Dill looked up over the file folder at Bill.

"Have you seen or talked to Agent Stallingsworth?" asked Dill.

"Not recently. I have him reporting to me via phone daily. The office Caller-ID® shows his home phone number as where the call is originating from," replied Bill, stirring his coffee.

"Any way that he could be calling from somewhere else?"

"You mean like using a phone number scrambling device?"

"Yes."

"A possibility, yes, but highly unlikely since such devices are registered and have their own unique serial numbers."

"There is always the possibility that someone may have an unregistered device."

"True, but wouldn't that device advertise itself, so to speak, as being stolen?"

"How?" asked Dill, pulling out the note pad once again and removing the pen from the spiral binding.

"My understanding is, from the manufacturer of these devices, that a stolen or unregistered unit will send out its serial number to the receiving phone via beeps. Those beeps are interpreted as letters and numbers, sort of like the old pen registers from decades ago."

"You say these beeps are sent to the receiving phone?"

"Yes, and those beeps show up as letters and numbers. The machine will keep sending out these beeps until the company records the serial number when the device is used. The company then sends a relay signal back to the device that shuts off the beeps when the serial number has been confirmed."

"Okay, thought I might ask. Who is the first person that is on my list today?"

"It appears to be the armorer. He is waiting in the outer office for you."

"Send him in," replied Dill.

Bill picked up the receiver on the phone that was on his desktop and pushed the orange button on the phone itself.

"Yes?" said Bill's secretary.

"Send in the armorer."

"Yes, sir."

The line went dead and the door opened to Bill's office a short time later. The armorer stepped into the room and closed the doors behind him. He walked three steps up to Bill's desk and stood rigidly at attention. He turned his head to his left so that he could see Agent Dill. The armorer then returned his gaze back to Bill.

Bill looked up to see the armorer decked out in full battle gear. He was wearing his body armour underneath his black battle dress uniform. As Bill observed him further, Bill noted that he saw no less than eight guns on the armorer.

One gun was located on each hip, one gun on each outside edge of the thigh, one gun each in the shoulder holster he was wearing under both arms. Next, as the armorer bent over to drop off one of the packages he was carrying on Bill's desktop, Bill could see the hammers of two more guns on his back.

"Armorer, reporting as ordered, sir, and I have your weapon from the armory along with the magazines and shoulder holster," he said, almost mechanically.

"Very well. Do you know why you were summoned to my office today?" asked Bill, taking the weapon and putting it on.

"Yes, sir, I do. I am to speak with Agent Dill of Internal Affairs, Miami, Florida office."

"That is correct. Agent Dill, do you have any questions for this person?" asked Bill, turning his head towards Dill.

"Yes. For the record, state your name and your job title here at the Denver office of the State Department," said Agent Dill, as he pulled out the note pad and removed the pen from the spiral binding.

"I am Special SPOT Agent Richtofen. I am currently serving the position as the chief armorer for the SPOT unit assigned to Denver," he responded.

"What do you in that capacity as chief armorer?"

"I am in charge of cleaning, maintenance, repair and replacement of both the shooting range and its associated equipment as well as the firearms that are stored in my armory."

"How long have you been in your current position?"

"12 years, 10 months, 22 days, sir."

"How many firearms do you have in your armory right now?"

"110 of them, sir. That count includes all shotguns, handguns, rifles, machine guns, grenade launchers and those firearms that are either being repaired or are checked out."

"Very good. Did you bring the printout I asked you to produce?"

"Yes, sir, right here," Richtofen said, and handed Agent Dill a two-inch thick printout.

"Thank you, you are dismissed for now. After I have reviewed this printout, I reserve the right to call you back again."

"Yes, sir. I will be down in my armory."

"You are dismissed," said Bill.

Special SPOT Agent Richtofen left the room and went back downstairs to his armory. The next person that Agent Dill was going to call into Bill's office was the Director of Personnel for the State Department's Denver office. Agent Dill completed up some notes and then turned to the next blank page in the note pad. He then merely nodded at Bill to send the next person into the office. Bill picked up the receiver once again and pushed the orange button.

"Yes?" said his secretary.

"You can send in the Director of Personnel."

"Yes, sir."

A moment later, the double doors to the office opened and in walked the Director of Personnel for the State Department in Denver. He came in, shut the doors behind him and stood in front of Agent Dill. Agent Dill looked up into his face and found it almost intimidating. The man's face was expressionless and his eyes were slate gray. Dill looked down at his note pad before beginning the questioning.

"Director of Personnel, reporting as ordered, sir," said the man in a deep, heavy voice.

"Do you know why I summoned you here today?"

"Yes, sir."

"How long have you served in your current position?"

"Six years, five months, ten days, sir."

"Do you have the printout that I asked you to bring?"

"Yes, sir."

He handed over a small printout to Dill. He looked it over and placed the printout into the file folder for this investigation. Dill continued to write down some notes while the Director of Personnel stood rigidly in front of him. After a few minutes, Dill looked back up at the man.

"I have no further questions to ask you at this time. However, I reserve the right to recall you," said Dill.

"I understand. I will make myself available in my office; just call me."

"I will. You can go now."

The Director of Personnel left the office. As Dill started looking over the printouts, he looked at his watch. It was 0915 hours. He knew that Michael wasn't due in until 0945 hours. During this short time period, Dill looked over the printouts and set them back down on the table that Bill had provided him. Dill had just poured himself a cup of coffee and had returned to his table, when Bill handed Dill a document.

Dill took the document and opened it up. There, before Dill, were

Michael's statements of what he had overheard that day. It also included the notes taken by Agent Hollister on Michael's whereabouts as well as who Michael was seeing. Dill added this to the file folder and looked up at Bill.

"Bill, you stated to me when I arrived here that you think these killings are being done by somebody on the inside, is that right?" asked Dill.

"Yes, I do believe that the killings are connected to the newly formed SPOT unit. As I provided to you on page 19 of that document, the picture is indeed of Osama Bin Laden and he is carrying something."

"So your theory is that during *Operation Bunker Buster,* Agent Stallingsworth sided with the 'enemy', in this case terrorists, to kill his own people and yet, he survived? This was done, according to your theory, to protect Osama Bin Laden. Is that correct as well?"

"Yes, that is correct."

"What makes you think this picture is the reason why other SPOT agents are dying? Why not just simply eliminate Michael Pigeon?"

"Then, try and explain away these facts. If you were a well-known terrorist and were captured alive, knowing that you would face a possible war crimes tribunal, what would you do? You would want to make sure that absolutely no one could identify you, wouldn't you? Also, you would want to ensure that any pictures of you were eliminated as well?"

"Sounds reasonable; go on."

"If there are no recent photographs of you floating around and you can eliminate the only people that can positively identify you at a trial, then how can a court of law convict you of a crime?"

"Sounds good so far. I want to talk to Agent Stallingsworth this afternoon and could I borrow Agent Pigeon for a special project this afternoon?"

"Sure, anything you want, just let me know. I am not going to interfere with your investigation. I'll call Agent Stallingsworth right now."

Bill reached over and grabbed his list of phone numbers. He tried his house first and received no answer. Bill then moved to the cell phone and was able to get a hold of him. Agent Stallingsworth told Bill that he would be in there to speak to Agent Dill at 1400 hours today if that was all right with Agent Dill.

Bill wrote the time down on a piece of paper that he had from a note pad sitting on the left, lower corner of his desktop. Agent Dill looked over the note and gave a thumb up sign that indicated the time was okay. Just then, the orange button lit up. Bill hung up the phone and pushed the button.

"Yes?" said Bill.

"Agent Michael Pigeon is out here, sir."

"Send him in, please."

"Yes, sir."

Michael entered the room and closed the doors behind him. Next, he locked the doors and then removed the phone cord from Bill's desk phone. He then pulled out a small black box from the front, left pocket of his pants. He turned it on and scanned the room with it.

No flashing red light on the box; Michael took the extra precautions of closing the curtains in the office, turning on the lights and finally turning on the radio that was in Bill's office. Michael tuned the dial to a loud rock-n-roll station and turned up the volume. Both Bill and Dill looked at each other before Michael spoke.

"Couldn't take any chances on that traitor secretary of yours giving away something vital from this inquisition," said Michael.

"Very good, Mr. Pigeon. I am most impressed with your security knowledge. How long have you been a SPOT agent?" asked Dill, completely ignoring the slightly loud music in the room as he pulled out his note pad and pen.

"A couple of years now. I have only gone on one mission where I lost some of my team," replied Michael.

"Yes, I have a copy of that report. Do you know who provided the helicopter to you?"

"Yes, it was a gift from a powerful friend of the Secretary of State as I understood it from Bill."

"Why did you turn on that horrible music?!" yelled Bill.

"I have a theory that last night, someone overheard my conversation on my cell phone from the third floor of my apartment. I'm reasonably certain that whoever overheard my conversation is the same one who killed Jeannie before I arrived." At saying her name, he almost broke down into tears again.

"I understand that you and Jeannie were getting perhaps close to each other?" asked Dill.

"Yes. Everything we did was strictly professional. I listened to one of her conversations really close and gathered that she hated males in general."

"You're correct according to her personal traits test she took. Now, I have to say that I don't suspect you of doing the killings."

"That's a good thing to know," said Michael irritably.

"However, I was wondering if you wanted to assist in catching whomever is responsible for the killings."

"I would be very interested in doing that. When do I start?"

"Today. Take your time with this part of the mission."

"What is it that you want me to do?"

"I want you to go to the records vault and fully review the file on *Operation Blue Ball.* I want you to read it thoroughly and then I want you to type up a summation of the operation in two parts."

"What are the two parts?"

"First, I want you to read the file from front to back. The first part is the objective analysis of the operation. I want to know what you think happened during the mission. The second part is a little harder."

"How much harder?"

"In the second part of the summation, I want you to read the file from front to back again. This time, I want you to read between the lines, if you know what I mean."

"I know what you mean. Then I suppose you want me to give a summation report based upon what isn't in writing in the file, right?"

"That's exactly what I want you to do. By the way, do you have any theories as to who is killing your team off?"

"No. I have reasonable suspicion that it's Agent Stallingsworth and Bill's no good secretary out there."

"What makes you think that?" asked Bill, rather incredulously.

"You're no good traitor secretary was one of the people that Agent Stallingsworth talked to that day I overheard their conversation."

"I have a copy of your statement, Michael, you don't need to go over it again."

"She's taken blood money to sell us out. In fact, I wouldn't be a bit surprised if she was either directly or indirectly involved with the failure of our first mission as a team. I think she's the one who should be talked to right now, not me!" yelled Michael.

"Michael, please try and keep a hold of yourself. Agent Dill is in the room," pleaded Bill.

"Its okay, Bill, I expected Michael to react this away. In fact, his reaction is not uncommon. How do you think the secretary out there is involved with the killings?"

"Other than my statement that I gave Bill earlier this month, I don't have any other proof. Although I made a statement to her earlier this week that made her very nervous."

"What makes you think that you made her nervous?"

"After I made my statement to her, she became very hostile towards me over the next few days. She was irritated with me at my mere presence. She also is very good friends with Agent Stallingsworth."

"You might have something there. Please carry out your part of the mission and report directly back to me."

"I will."

Michael smiled, turned off the radio and opened the curtains. He then unlocked the doors and plugged the phone back into the wall. As he exited the office, he turned to Bill's secretary and whispered into her ear once again.

"If I find out you had anything to do with my team being killed off, this includes either a direct or an indirect hand in it, I will shove the barrel of my .357 Magnum up your vagina and pull the trigger."

At this he pulled away from her and left her standing there in the outer office. She was shaken and then angry with herself. Michael knew that this might have caused a reaction in her. Quickly, so that she didn't see him, he ducked down behind the filing cabinets and waited. Sure enough, a few seconds later, after she thought Michael had left the outer office, she picked up the phone and dialed Agent Stallingsworth's cell phone number.

"You need to kill Michael tonight. He has just threatened me," she said, all flustered.

"Well, what did he say to you?" asked Agent Stallingsworth.

"He said, 'If I find out you had anything to do with the killing of my team, I will shove the barrel of my .357 Magnum up your vagina and pull the trigger.'"

"You can disregard that statement. He wouldn't kill anyone unless it was his only option. However, I am moving up the list towards him. I have one female and one male left to kill."

"Well, you need to hurry up with Michael's demise."

"I'll take it under advisement. How about going for drinks tonight after work?"

"Sure, sounds like fun. Where do you want me to meet you?"

"The *Blue Oyster* bar and grill over off of Federal Drive and 104th street."

"Sounds good, what time?"

"6:00 p.m. sounds good to me. We can talk and enjoy happy hour."

"See you then."

She hung up the phone as Michael started to walk off down the hallway. He turned to his right and yelled back down the hallway to the outer office.

"Traitor!"

She spun around looking for the body that belonged to the voice, but Michael was long gone. He was headed into the basement to the records vault. He arrived at the records vault and knocked on the cage door. The records vault technician looked up over the top of some files she had and smiled at him. A moment later, he heard the buzzing sound that indicated the door was unlocked for him. He opened the door, stepped into the vault and shut the door behind him.

"What can I do for you Michael?" she asked as she set down the files on the top of a short filing cabinet.

"I need to look at the file folder for *Operation Blue Ball.*"

"Sure. That operation took place eight years ago and is in Area 4, Section F," she said.

"Thank you very much," replied Michael, as he headed off to the lower sections of the records vault.

For Michael, it was going to be a long night tonight. He found the file folder on *Operation Blue Ball* and started reading through the file. The words of Agent Dill came back to him while he was reading it for the first time. Michael looked around and found a notebook and some pens lying around on the next table over. He picked them up and started making his notes from which he would make his report for Agent Dill. Michael didn't leave the vault until almost 2200 hours. He was tired and went straight home to bed.

CHAPTER 5

▼

Michael rolled over in bed and shut off the alarm clock. After rubbing his eyes a little bit, he rose up in bed. He looked out his apartment window and saw the dawning of the day. The sky was overcast and the gray of the clouds almost matched his gray mood. He bowed his head slightly and closed his eyes tightly for a few seconds and said a silent prayer for all the SPOT agents who had been killed over the last month. After this, he stepped out of bed and took a shower.

After the shower, he put on his shoulder holster and went out the door. He locked the door to his apartment and looked around carefully at his surroundings. Nothing seemed out of place, but Michael still couldn't help feeling like he was being watched. Little did he realize that Agent Stallingsworth was the one who was watching his every move.

Stallingsworth glared at Michael through the binoculars he had used to watch him. Stallingsworth was studying Michael carefully for any signs of weakness. Since he had not found any today, he went about his preparations for this evening's killing; Agent Gomez was going to die tonight.

Michael walked out to his car, did his customary check for explosive devices and then stepped into the car. He started up the engine and drove to the parking garage. After parking the car, he stepped out of it and locked the door. As he looked around the garage, it seemed deserted. Michael started walking towards the elevators, when he heard a noise.

Instinctively, he dropped down to get out of the way of possible bullets and he drew his own weapon out. Next he started scanning quickly all the way around him, looking for what made the noise. He walked carefully towards one of the many trashcans in the garage and saw it moving around. Carefully he approached the still moving trashcan and slowly peered inside.

He found an alley cat inside the trashcan. It was black and its fur coat had a strange sheen to it like it hadn't had a bath in several months. He pursed his lips together and put up his weapon, cursing under his breath at his own imagination making him act like a fool.

As he turned around, Agent Dill appeared out of nowhere and was standing beside Michael. Michael hadn't heard him walk up during all this excitement. Michael noticed that Agent Dill was putting his gun up as well.

"Good morning, Agent Dill, did you get a good laugh out of me today?" asked Michael, sarcastically.

"No, I didn't laugh at all. In fact, I heard the same noise you did. I was coming up the stairs from the parking level under this one. I saw you approaching the trashcan and thought that since you had your gun out, maybe I should have mine out as well."

"Sorry, I didn't know what, or whom, it was that had made the noise," replied Michael, feeling rather foolish.

"It's okay, it happens to the best of us sometimes. Especially when we are under lots of stress. By the way, what caused the noise?"

"I discovered an alley cat in the trashcan and I suspect that the cat has not had a bath in several months."

"What makes you think that?"

"The cat's fur coat had a bright sheen to it from being so dirty."

"Very observant Michael. Have you had a chance to complete the assignment I gave you?"

"I have a few more pages of the file to look over before I type up my report."

"Did you finish all the project off?"

"No, just the first part. I'm going to reread the file today and see if there is something that I might have missed."

"Very good. I gather that you will be in the records vault then?"

"Yes, for most of the morning anyways."

"Stop by Bill's office and get some coffee before you go down there, okay?"

"Yes, sir, I will."

Michael let Agent Dill walk over to the elevators. Dill pushed the call button and Michael waited until Dill had stepped into the elevator and disappeared before walking over to the elevator himself. Michael pushed the call button for the elevator and waited. When the elevator arrived, the doors opened and Michael stepped into the elevator, pushing the button for the eighth floor.

A few minutes later, the doors opened and he stepped out onto a very busy floor. He then walked down the hallway to Bill's office. He passed by Bill's secretary, who gave him an evil look before going back to typing up some memorandums, before entering Bill's office. Once he was inside, Michael shut the double-doors and locked them.

"Mr. Pigeon, I have just completed reading over Agent Hollister's notes that he wrote about you. Your flying lessons were interrupted by this investigation and I would like to say, sorry for the inconvenience," said Agent Dill, as he set down the file folder on the tabletop.

Michael, who had been pouring himself a cup of coffee, stopped pouring the coffee and turned around to look at Dill. Bill, as Michael found out, was totally oblivious to the conversation as he was on the phone with the Secretary of State. Michael, slightly perplexed by the whole statement, turned back around to face the coffee pot. He picked up a plastic spoon and started stirring his coffee.

"Thank you for your apology, Agent Dill. My flying lessons were put on hold until the outcome of this investigation brings to justice those parties responsible for the deaths of my coworkers."

"According to Agent Hollister, your flying lessons are important to you."

"Yes, they are important to me, however, I do have duties here that require my attention. Now, if you will excuse me, I have a report to type and print up for you."

"Take all the time you need."

"I will. By the way, how many SPOT agents are still alive?"

"Three. You, Mr. Gomez, and Miss Everett."

"Let me get that report done for you."

Michael left the office, glared at the secretary like she had done to him earlier, and walked down the hallway. He yelled back down the hallway at her, "Traitor!" He then pushed the call button and when the elevator arrived, he stepped into it.

He then pushed the button for the basement level where the records vault was located. When the elevator doors opened for the last time, Michael stepped out of the elevator and walked down the dimly lit hallway. He soon arrived at the caged door and knocked. The records vault technician looked up and buzzed him through the door. Michael didn't say anything to her, but continued on his way to the computer area.

When he arrived at the computer area, he sat down at one of the 10 terminals that were in there. Next, he pulled out a compact disc and placed it into the CD tray slot of the computer case. The computer started reading the disc and found that there was only one file on the disc. Michael used the mouse to point and click on the file that he wanted printed.

In a few minutes, the laser jet printer behind him spit out the four-page document. Once he had the printout in hand, he went back up in the elevator to Bill's office. He handed the document to Dill and left the room without saying a word.

Michael returned back down to the records vault and opened the file back up on *Operation Blue Ball*. He went over the file once again, page by page. He read and then reread every page. After a few hours, he closed the file folder back up and went to lunch.

When he returned from lunch, he finished off reading the file. As he put the file folder back on the shelf, his mind refused to let a small discrepancy in the file go unnoticed. His mind was telling him to take the file folder back down off the shelf and look at it again.

He pulled the file folder down off the shelf once more. He took it to the same table that he had just been at and sat down in the chair. Rubbing his eyes a little, he opened the file folder back up and reread the whole file from start to finish. He had closed the file folder back up, when a nagging discrepancy lodged into his mind. Grabbing a pen and a note pad that was already on the table, Michael wrote down what the discrepancy was and put it into the report he was writing.

After dinner, Michael went back down into the records vault for the last time that evening. He typed up his report as part of the second phase of Dill's plan. After typing up the report, Michael printed it out and deleted it off the computer. He turned the computer off, since he was the only one down there at this time of the night. Michael left the records vault and went to Bill's office.

Bill's secretary was gone, but Michael could hear Bill and Dill talking to each other. He knocked on the double-doors and then entered the office. After entering the office, he locked the double-doors and marched right over to Dill. Michael handed Dill his one paragraph report of eight sentences. Dill looked it over and smiled.

Unknown to Michael, Michael had discovered a small enough discrepancy to get noticed by Dill's expert eyes. Now, Dill was going to start turning his attention towards Agent Stallingsworth. Dill dismissed Michael with the wave of his right hand. Michael unlocked the double-doors and left the room. Dill smiled and looked over at Bill.

"Michael Pigeon is an excellent SPOT agent, Bill. He knows how to follow instructions," said Dill.

"His following instructions exactly to the letter was one of the reasons why I chose him to be a SPOT agent and one of the main reasons why I placed him in charge of the SPOT team," replied Bill, with a hint of pleasure in his voice.

"Michael found something that may be a clue to solving these murders."

"Oh, what did he find?"

"A discrepancy that needs to be followed up on. I will need to speak to the armorer again in the morning."

"I'll call him at home right now and let him know."

"Have a good evening, Bill."

"You do the same, Agent Dill."

Bill picked up the receiver and dialed the armorer's home phone number. He answered the phone and stated that he would be able to speak to Agent Dill first thing in the morning. As Bill hung up the phone and prepared to go home for the evening, Agent Stallingsworth was preparing to kill again.

The overcast sky helped hide Agent Stallingsworth very well. Agent Gomez came out of the little Mexican cantina in Wheatridge, Colorado and stepped into his car. Agent Stallingsworth waited for Agent Gomez to drive by before Stallingsworth started his own car up.

Cautiously, Stallingsworth followed Agent Gomez. Agent Gomez lived in a small apartment complex. Stallingsworth watched as Gomez parked his car and stepped out of it. As Gomez walked up the steps into his apartment, Stallingsworth parked his car and stepped out of it.

Stallingsworth grabbed his little black bag for tonight's killing and smiled at himself in the side-view mirror of his car. Dressed in black except for his face, which he quickly covered in a ski mask, he blended in perfectly with the shadows cast by the overcast skies. Occasional lightening would light up the sky followed by thunder, but no one would see him tonight. Carefully, he opened the door and walked down the stairs to Agent Gomez's apartment.

Setting down the black bag and opening it up, Stallingsworth removed a lock picking kit and started picking at the lock. Within a few seconds, he had defeated the doorknob lock. As Stallingsworth turned the doorknob ever so slowly, he met resistance in the form of the deadbolt lock. Carefully he closed the door and then picked that lock as well.

He opened the door quickly and stepped inside. He listened closely for any signs that he had been detected entering the apartment. The only sounds were coming from a radio, tuned to a radio station that played Mexican music and the shower was running.

For Stallingsworth, this was better than he expected. He set the black bag down on the living room floor. Slowly, he removed his weapon and put the silencer on the end of the barrel. He screwed the silencer on the barrel tightly and then double-checked the weapon and the magazine. Both were ready to go for tonight. All Stallingsworth had to do was wait for Gomez to step out of the shower.

He didn't have to wait long, for just a few minutes later, the water stopped. As Gomez stepped out of the shower and opened the bathroom door, his eyes went wide and his mouth dropped open at seeing an intruder in his apartment.

Coolly, Stallingsworth shot him to death. He put seven rounds into the torso area. He then put one round into Gomez's throat and another round, at close range, into his head, right between the eyes.

After the shooting was completed, Stallingsworth waited for a few minutes to make sure that Gomez was dead and that no one had heard the noise of him falling onto the floor. When he could hear nothing,

Stallingsworth went to work on Gomez. Carefully he removed the evidence that he had been there.

As he grabbed the black bag and exited the apartment, Stallingsworth was going to celebrate again tonight. Stallingsworth closed the door behind him and walked back to his car. He then drove to the warehouse and destroyed the evidence.

The next morning, Michael woke up and found sunlight streaming through his bedroom window. As he rolled over in bed, he heard a knock at his door. Thinking that this might be a booby trap, he jumped out of bed. Quickly he put on his bathrobe and grabbed his pistol that was sitting on the nightstand next to his bed.

He approached the door and unlocked it after peering out the peephole and seeing no one. Leaving the chain on the door as a stopgap measure, he opened it up slowly. He started to inch the barrel of his pistol out the door and Agent Everett stopped dead in her tracks.

"Excuse me, Michael, but is that really necessary?" she asked, nervously.

"No. I'm sorry, I didn't know it was you."

Michael put the gun back up and returned a short time later to open up the door. As he opened up the door and let Agent Everett into his apartment, Michael could tell something was wrong. Clad only in his bathrobe, he offered a chair at the kitchen table for her to sit down. He rummaged around the kitchen and managed to find some coffee. After starting coffee, he turned around to face Agent Everett.

"What's on your mind Agent Everett?" asked Michael.

"You know, Jeannie was right, you do have a nice body," she said.

The mention of the name brought back some pain like being stabbed in the eye with a hot poker. The feeling passed away shortly and he started smiling again.

"Why, thank you, Agent Everett, for your compliment. However, I don't think you came over here to discuss my physique, did you?"

"No. I think something's wrong with Agent Gomez."

"Okay, what gave you that idea?"

"We were supposed to have breakfast this morning and he never showed up at the coffee shop we usually meet at. I called him on both his home and his cell phone and no answer."

"Well, let's have some coffee and then we'll both go over to his apartment and see if he is all right."

"That sounds great."

After coffee, Michael changed into some better clothing and rode with Agent Everett over to Agent Gomez's apartment. When they had entered the complex parking lot, Michael developed a sudden twinge that they were going to find Agent Gomez dead. When they had parked the car, they both stepped out of the car and walked down the steps to Gomez's apartment. Michael knocked and that's when he found the door opened up slightly.

Quickly, Michael drew his weapon out of the shoulder holster. Kicking the door open, he scanned the room with his gun. As he took a few steps into the apartment, he heard a stifled scream from behind him.

Turning around, he looked at Agent Everett. She was holding her left hand over her mouth and was pointing frantically at the floor by Michael's feet with her right hand. Michael looked down and saw the bloody body of Agent Gomez. Michael reholstered his weapon and knelt down over Gomez. He felt for a pulse, but didn't find one.

"Agent Everett, do you have your cell phone on you?"

"Yes," she said, taking her left hand away from her mouth.

"Call 911 and then call Bill."

"Okay," she said, as she reached into her purse and pulled out her cell phone while walking away from the apartment and the terrible scene from within.

Meanwhile, Bill, Dill and the armorer were in Bill's office. Dill was going over the report that Michael had given him the day before. Bill was on the phone once again with various people and was oblivious to the conversation that Dill was having with the armorer.

The armorer was looking a little nervous as Dill looked over Michael's report one last time and then set it down on the tabletop. Next, Dill withdrew his note pad and pulled out the pen from the spiral binding.

"What is a Form 1464 used for in your office?" asked Dill.

"Oh, a Form 1464 is the form that I am required to fill out when any government issued property or equipment, in this case a weapon, has been lost, stolen or damaged. This includes weapons that were damaged or destroyed while on missions," replied the armorer, confidently.

"I see. How many SPOT agents, excluding Michael Pigeon, have had or ever have had a .45 ACP weapon issued to them?"

"Five. One is dead, one is retired and took it with him after completing Forms 4373 and 4551, and one reported his as being destroyed with the Form 1464. One is in this room right now and I am the other one."

"Do you have the serial number and the owner's name on the one pistol that was claimed on this Form 1464?"

"Yes. Let me go through my archive files and I will make you a copy. Fair enough?"

"I look forward to hearing from you today."

The armorer left as Bill, scribbling down some information on a note pad, looked over at Dill with very concerned eyes. Dill looked down at the note pad and saw that another killing had occurred. Bill did what he was supposed to do and dispatched the crime scene personnel.

After Bill hung up the phone, the armorer, handing Dill some paperwork, briefly interrupted him. Dill looked over the paperwork and put the copy in the file.

"Another killing, Bill?" asked Dill.

"Yes, Agent Gomez was found just a few minutes ago by Agents Pigeon and Everett. When will this stop?" pleaded Bill.

"Very soon. I think I know who has been doing the killings," replied Agent Dill, confidently.

CHAPTER 6

▼

The police released both Michael and Agent Everett after they gave their statements to them. He walked back to Agent Everett's car and they both stepped into her car. Calmly, they drove back to Michael's place in total silence. Michael was about to say something, when his cell phone rang. He looked down at the number that came up and saw that it was Bill calling him from his office.

"Hello, Bill what can I do for you?" asked Michael, without putting much feeling behind the question.

"Well, it's good to hear your voice. Look, Agent Dill wants you to come into the office right away. He's got another special project for you to do."

"I'll be in, in about an hour."

"See you then."

Bill hung up the phone as he looked across the desk at Agent Dill.

"Do you think you know who is doing the killings?" asked Bill.

"No, I don't have any definite suspects, yet. However, both the second report that I received from Michael and the paperwork from the armorer tell me I'm on the right track. I just need someone to do some more foot work."

"I sure hope you're right. I don't have too many more SPOT agents left."

"I know you don't. However, this investigation is entering a critical phase. I cannot afford to gather the information myself or else the suspect will get away with the murders because I poisoned the evidence gathering."

"Can't I do more?"

"Yes, call the SPOT agent switchboard and inform them that you are implementing procedure 050."

"Okay."

Once again Agent Dill went over the file folder. Dill asked Bill to call the armorer once again. Bill dialed the armorer's internal extension number and asked him to come up to the office right away. A few minutes later, the armorer arrived in Bill's office. Agent Dill pulled out his note pad and removed the pen from the spiral binding.

"What is the normal procedure, generally speaking, of repairing damaged weapons?" asked Dill.

"The correct procedure in accordance with State Department Policy and Procedures Manual, Chapter 22, Firearms, Section 112, Firearms Repair and or Replacement, is to send the weapon back to the manufacturer for the repair."

"Why send the weapon back to the manufacturer?"

"That is the policy of the federal government, sir. I don't ask why."

"You're right, you shouldn't ask why. Do you keep some sort of record of this?"

"Yes, sir. I believe you are referring to the weapon that was reported by Agent Stallingsworth as being lost, stolen or damaged, am I correct?"

"Yes, I was wondering about that particular one."

"I anticipated that this might be the one, so I brought along the paperwork."

The armorer handed Dill a piece of paper. Dill dismissed him as Bill got off the phone with the SPOT switchboard. To Dill, Bill seemed more relaxed. Michael soon showed up. Again, upon entering the office, he locked the double-doors and closed the curtains. He then stood in front of Agent Dill.

"Michael, how about a little vacation?" asked Dill.

"How long and where?" asked Michael in return.

"I want you to go to the city of Springfield, Massachusetts and make an appointment to see the armorer who repaired a certain Smith and Wesson firearm that was supposedly sent to them eight and half years ago."

"When should I leave?"

"The sooner the better."

Michael was soon armed with the information that he needed to conduct this most crucial part of the investigation. Michael went home, packed a small duffle bag full of clothes and headed to the airport. Along the way, he stopped by the armory in the building and dropped off his weapon.

Soon, he was landing in Massachusetts. He rented a car and drove to a local hotel for the evening. The next morning, he called Smith and Wesson and asked for an appointment with the armorer that had repaired the weapon.

Michael had breakfast and then drove to the Smith and Wesson plant. He signed into the visitor's logbook and sat down in the waiting area. Soon, a small man came out the door in front of Michael and motioned for Michael to follow him.

As they walked down the hallway, Michael was able to see the manufacturing processes of various weapons. As they entered a small office, the man shut the door and locked it. Michael sat down when the man sat down.

"Mr. Pigeon, you do understand that without a search warrant or a subpoena of some kind I cannot divulge certain information to you," said the man.

"I understand that completely."

"However, I received a subpoena duces tecum via my fax line this morning. I have been instructed to fully cooperate with you."

"Great, I'm glad I'm so efficient," said Michael, trying to figure out how all this paperwork had arrived without him knowing about it.

"What is it you wish to know about the weapon?"

"Who is the armorer who repaired it?"

"I am. To make sure that we are talking about the same weapon, could you please give me the serial number?"

"The serial number that I have is VBF6903."

"I remember that weapon. The weapon in question, by the serial number that you just gave me, is a third generation Smith and Wesson®

Model 4506-1. It was manufactured March 11, 1988 and was purchased by the government on May 4, 1988."

Michael was most impressed by this person's knowledge. Michael began to take notes using the pen-like device that was in his right, front jacket pocket. The pen-like device was really a digital recorder. Michael turned it on and asked the man to repeat what he had just said. As the digital recorder recorded the conversation, Michael only interrupted to ask clarifying questions.

"So, this weapon was returned to you for a repair then?" asked Michael.

"Yes, it was."

"What was the nature of the repair?"

"The weapon's problem was twofold. The pistol had taken an armor piercing round to the chamber area. Then, as I found out, someone had tried to screw on a silencer."

"Tried to screw on a silencer?" asked Michael.

"Yes. Normally, our barrels are not designed for screw on type silencers. Most silencers today are the magnetic type or are put on over the barrel and have screws on the silencer itself with which the user can attach it to the gun."

"Okay. So did you repair the damage?"

"Yes. But it was expensive and time consuming. We had to melt down the weapon itself and repour it into the proper mold. After that, we were able to remove the silencer and melted down the barrel as well. Once this was completed, we were able to repour the barrel."

"Did you put the same serial number on the weapon when it was repoured?"

"Yes. By law, unless the firearm is totally destroyed by, say, a fire or some other catastrophe, the firearm's unique serial number can be transferred to the new firearm provided that it meets the requirements of Title 18, United States Code, as Amended, Section 19 on Firearms."

"In this case, the new firearm met those requirements then?"

"Yes. In accordance with Paragraph 234, Section I at that time. Since that time, we can now declare if a weapon should be destroyed for safety reasons. If we should decide that the weapon has to be destroyed for safety reasons, then there is a whole lot of paperwork we must do before the firearm is destroyed."

"I see. What did you do with the weapon after you completely restored it, so to speak?"

"We returned it to the federal government agency that had sent it to us in the first place."

"Were there any modifications done to this new firearm?"

"Strange you should ask that question. Yes, there were some modifications done to this new firearm."

"What sort of modifications?"

"Night sights were installed and in addition to the new factory barrel, another barrel was requested to be sent with it back to the government."

"What kind of a barrel?"

"A threaded type for attaching threaded type silencers."

"Do you by chance have the paperwork requesting that extra barrel?"

"Yes, it should be here in the archive files."

As the man started rooting through the archive files, Michael was getting more and more nervous. He was getting nervous because he had a nagging suspicion in the back of his mind that Agent Stallingsworth was the one doing the killings. The man finally found the file and walked across the hallway to make a copy of the repair order.

He returned a short time later and gave Michael a copy of the paperwork. Michael looked at the names on the repair order. Agent Stallingsworth was listed as the owner of the weapon and then under Secretary of State, Lillian Winks signed off on the repair order as the "authorized agent for the requesting agency."

"By any chance do you have the ballistics report on that weapon?" asked Michael on a long shot.

"No. The government didn't make keeping a test fired slug from the weapon a part of the weapon's history until 1998."

"I understand, just thought I would ask. Thank you, sir, you have been a very big help today."

"Any time."

Michael shook the man's hand and then returned to his hotel room. Immediately, he packed up his clothes and checked out. He hailed a taxi to take him to the airport. Michael was able to find three late night flights with either a stop in Denver or Denver was the final stop. He boarded the airplane and was soon landing in Denver.

Michael arrived at his apartment at 0415 hours at which time he double locked his front door and double locked his sliding glass door. He went to bed and didn't wake up until late in the morning, when his phone started ringing.

He stumbled into the kitchen and answered the phone. Bill was at the other end of the line. Michael figured Agent Dill was in the room as well.

"Good morning, Michael. I didn't expect you back so soon. Is everything all right?" asked Bill.

Michael could detect a hint of nervousness in his voice.

"Yes, everything went all right. In fact, it went better than expected. I will be coming into the office this afternoon with some interesting news for Agent Dill."

"That's great. Now, Michael, please don't lie to me when I ask you this question," said Bill, who then placed the phone conversation on the speakerphone so that Agent Dill could hear both the question and the answer.

"I have no reason to lie to you, Bill. Has something happened?"

"Yes and no. Agent Dill and myself are trying to find out exactly what happened last night."

"Bill, I'm happy to answer any question that you ask me."

"That's good. Where were you last night between 0100 hours and 0500 hours?"

"Is that Mountain Standard Time or Eastern Standard Time?"

"Mountain Standard Time."

"Well, at 0100 hours, Mountain Standard Time, I was in a security check line at the Springfield, Massachusetts Airport trying to get a late night flight home. I boarded United Airlines Flight 2020 at or about 0130 hours. I don't remember what time the plane took off because I had other things on my mind."

"I understand, Michael you're doing just fine. Please, continue."

Bill looked over at Agent Dill who was smiling and taking down notes.

"The plane landed at 0330 hours in Denver and I arrived at my apartment at 0415 hours."

"Thank you. Now, I'm going to put you on a secure phone line for the other questions."

"Okay by me, Bill."

Bill punched a few buttons and soon the red LED light was no longer flashing. Bill took in a deep breath and let it out slowly.

"Michael, did you take any weapons with you to Massachusetts?"

"No. I left my weapons in the armory just before I took off. In fact, that was the day before yesterday at or about 1905 hours."

"Okay. I trust you. Now, did you make a threatening statement to my secretary at any time this week or even in the past about being a traitor, being paid blood money or 'I'll kill you,' etc.?"

"Yes, I have made such a statement like that this week."

"Mr. Pigeon, when was the last time you fired your .357 magnum?" asked Agent Dill.

"It has been at least three weeks, maybe more."

"Would you recognize your weapon if you saw it?" asked Agent Dill again.

"Yes, I would. Is there something wrong?"

"Mr. Pigeon, would you please come into the office right now," said Agent Dill.

"I'll be right down there."

Michael hung up the phone and Bill hung up his receiver as well. Bill looked across the desktop at Agent Dill. Bill was apprehensive right now. The murder weapon, found at the scene of the gruesome killing, was marked as Exhibit "A" with a yellow tag attached to it. The barrel was coated in blood and the cylinder was showing one spent cartridge.

When Michael arrived, he noticed that Bill's secretary wasn't in her usual spot to glare at him. Michael walked through the outer office and into Bill's office. Carefully he closed the double-doors and locked them. As he turned back around, he saw Agent Dill holding up a nickel-plated .357 magnum that looked an awful lot like his own that was down in the armory.

"Michael, do you have issued to you, or do you own, a .357 magnum revolver?" asked Agent Dill, as he pulled out his note pad once again. With pen in hand he started to take notes.

"Yes, I was issued a .357 magnum revolver for my training," replied Michael confidently.

"Would you say that weapon lying there on the desktop is yours?" asked Agent Dill.

Michael looked at the revolver on the table. He looked at it carefully and then turned around to face Agent Dill.

"No, Agent Dill, that revolver on the desktop is not mine."

"How do you know?"

"My revolver has a six inch barrel on it, for starters."

"Anything else that would differentiate yours from this one on the desktop?"

"Mine has a blue barrel to it; no nickel-plating."

"What make and model is your revolver?"

"Taurus® Model 608B6."

"I thought so, Bill, he didn't kill your secretary. However, Michael, would you let me test your hands to see if you have fired a weapon recently?" asked Agent Dill, as he broke open the two swabs from the nitrite test kit.

He walked over and swabbed both of Michael's hands. The results were negative. Michael had not fired a weapon in several weeks, based upon only traces of the test coming up as orange. Agent Dill smiled as he turned back to Bill. Michael handed Agent Dill the paperwork from Smith and Wesson. Agent Dill looked over the paperwork, made a copy of it and then put it into the file folder.

"Michael, my secretary was killed last night. They found that revolver at the murder scene inside of her house in Westminster. The time of death was sometime between 0100 and 0500 hours this morning," said Bill.

"Let me guess, the revolver barrel was found inside her vagina?" asked Michael.

"Yes, it was," replied Bill.

"I kind of figured that was going to happen, sooner or later," said Michael.

"Why?" asked Dill.

"Bill's secretary and Agent Stallingsworth were really good friends."

"I see. Bill, based upon this evidence that I received from Michael today, I have probable cause to think that Agent Stallingsworth is the one who is systematically wiping out your SPOT unit," announced Agent Dill.

"We should get him right away," said Bill.

"I'll need Michael to go to the federal building and give his statement to the judge so that an arrest warrant can be issued."

"I understand. I just find it hard to believe that it was one of my own," said Bill, still rather shocked by the whole series of events.

"Well, we should be heading downtown now. Michael, you will need to come with me."

"Gladly. I just hope that Agent Stallingsworth doesn't slip through our fingers like he did with the FBI."

"I understand your frustration, Michael, but put it aside when you face the judge."

"Yes, sir, I will put my personal feelings aside."

In a few minutes, Michael and Agent Dill were standing in front of the Honorable Judge Shelly Houston. She was asking lots of questions of both Agent Dill and Agent Pigeon. She weighed her options and then asked both of them to step outside her chambers. They walked out and waited for nearly an hour before she called them back into her chambers. There, much to Agent Dill's relief was not only the arrest warrant for Agent Stallingsworth, but the search and seizure warrants for the firearm, the silencer and any related criminal evidence. Agent Dill scooped up the paperwork and they both quickly left the courthouse.

Michael was feeling a bit more relaxed now knowing that Agent Stallingsworth was about to be put behind bars for a long time to come if he was convicted. However, for Michael, he couldn't help but think about the possibility that if Stallingsworth knew he might be arrested, Stallingsworth would take to flight. He might even go to a country that had no extradition treaties with the United States and be out of reach forever. Michael waited until after Agent Dill had left before talking to Bill.

"Bill, if Agent Stallingsworth takes to flight, he gets away with murder," said Michael.

"If that becomes the case, then I will send you out to get him."

"Somehow, that's not very comforting,"

"Goodnight, Michael."

54

Michael left the building and went back to his apartment. Upon arriving at his front door, he found Agent Everett sitting there. He let her inside and double locked all the doors and this time, the windows. Until Agent Stallingsworth was caught, he wasn't taking any chances on his security.

CHAPTER 7

▼

Armed with the arrest warrant and the search and seizure warrants, Agent Dill, along with four other SPOT agents from the Denver field office, raided Agent Stallingsworth's house. When Dill found out that Stallingsworth wasn't home at the time, Dill used a portable battering ram to knock the door open. Once the door was open, he and the other SPOT agents burst into the living room. What they found horrified them.

The house was completely empty. No furniture, no nothing in the house. Agent Dill had the other SPOT agents search the house anyway. They searched the upper floors of the house as well as the basement. They came up empty handed as well. Dill knew what had happened, someone had tipped Stallingsworth off that there was going to be a raid at his house. Stallingsworth then, Dill surmised, vacated the place.

Dill had the trashcan outside searched for any clues as to where Stallingsworth might have fled. Nothing of any value was recovered. The other SPOT agents kept searching the local area for other clues. They found, in the garage, Stallingsworth's car. The telephone didn't work in the house either, as Agent Dill found out when he plugged in a small device that he carried in his left suit pocket to detect such things.

After about an hour of searching the grounds, the house and the surrounding forest area, Agent Dill decided to call it a finished project. As all the SPOT agents were leaving the premises, Agent Dill took one last look around the empty house and shut the door. He put a copy of the search and seizure warrants inside the house on the floor.

He then walked down the front steps to his car and stepped inside. Starting the car, he drove slowly to the downtown section of Denver. After parking in the garage and locking his car up, he took two steps towards the elevator, when the car that was parked to the left of his rolled down its window.

The person sitting in the passenger seat of the car calmly shot Agent Dill to death, or so he thought. Afterwards, instead of cleaning up the mess, Agent Stallingsworth took one last look at his handiwork and had the driver leave the parking garage. Agent Stallingsworth knew nobody had heard the shots, because the silencer had been attached to the pistol. As the car exited the parking garage, the driver took Stallingsworth to the airport where he boarded a chartered jet.

Stallingsworth had taken the time to close out all of his accounts and put the money into several suitcases. He took those suitcases out of the trunk of the car and walked up the ramp into the jet. Inside one of the suitcases, buried at the bottom of the pile of bills, was the murder weapon with the silencer still attached. The jet took off and made many stops along the way in 11 foreign countries. It was in one of those foreign countries that Stallingsworth entered.

The country that Stallingsworth had chosen, he chose wisely. He had done some work for most of the highest people in the government. They owed him a favor and he called them to tell them he was cashing in on that favor. They agreed to harbor him; in exchange they wanted some money.

Stallingsworth had brought nearly ten million U.S. dollars into the country with him. Upon entry into the country, he was picked up by some government figures and driven to his new home overlooking the bay area. He had also chosen this country because he knew they had no extradition treaties with the United States. He was home free, he thought, as he sat back in his lawn chair that was on the balcony and sipped his drink through a straw.

Meanwhile, Bill was becoming worried that the raid had gone wrong. It was nearly 1130 hours and still no word from Agent Dill. He had already received a report from the four other SPOT agents who assisted him with the raid. Bill was upset that Stallingsworth had escaped, but he was more concerned with why he had not received any word yet from Agent Dill. Bill thought by now that he would have received the phone call saying that Dill had caught Stallingsworth and that Stallingsworth was being processed into the criminal justice system. He continued to wait.

Meanwhile, Michael had arrived at work as usual and parked his car on the same parking level as Agent Dill had. Michael saw Agent Dill's car parked a few spots down the same row. Casually, Michael started walking down the row towards Dill's car.

As he arrived at the edge of Dill's car, he saw feet and a pool of blood next to Dill's car. Michael looked down and saw Agent Dill looking up blankly into the air. Michael looked around and saw a telephone nearby. He ran to the telephone and called 911.

Michael then returned to where Agent Dill was at to check for any signs of life. Michael felt Dill's left wrist and felt a weak pulse. To Michael, that was a good sign. As security personnel from the building's security department started to arrive along with the fire department and the ambulance personnel, Michael stood up to leave.

A weak, feeble right hand grabbed Michael's left ankle. Michael turned around to see what had grabbed him and saw Dill mouthing some words. He knelt down beside Dill so that he could hear what Dill had to say.

"Stallingsworth, don't let him get away with these killings," said Agent Dill in a raspy voice. Slowly he reached inside his right suit jacket pocket and pulled out the arrest warrant and handed it to Michael.

"I won't let him get away with it," replied Michael.

Suddenly, Dill tensed up and became relaxed. As Michael turned around, he saw the paramedics coming out of the elevator. The building security personnel quickly followed the paramedics. The building security personnel were being shoved out of the way by the fire department personnel and some Denver police officers.

Michael stepped out of their way very quickly. The paramedics went to work, while the police questioned Michael. After the police were through with Michael, he glanced over the police officer's left shoulder to see Agent Dill being carried out of the parking garage on a gurney.

Michael walked over to the elevator and pushed the call button.

After stepping into the elevator and the doors closed, he closed his eyes and said a silent prayer for Agent Dill. Michael thought that, in a way, Dill was the unlucky one of Stallingsworth's victims; Dill was alive.

When the elevator doors opened, Michael stepped out of the elevator and walked down the hallway towards Bill's office. As he stepped through the door into the outer office, a new face looked up at him from behind the desk where Bill's former secretary used to sit.

"Good morning, Mr. Pigeon, Bill is expecting you," said Agent Everett.

"Thank you," replied Michael as he walked passed her and opened the double-doors to Bill's office.

Michael walked in, shut the doors and locked them. He went about closing the curtains and even went so far as to turn on the radio once again. This time, however, the volume wasn't as loud as before and Michael had turned the dial to a radio station that played classical music. Bill nodded his head in appreciation of not being subjected to heavy metal rock-n-roll this time. Michael walked over and stood in front of Bill's desk, Michael's bottom lip was quivering.

"Good morning, Michael," said Bill not aware yet of the catastrophe downstairs.

"If you say so, Bill," said Michael, almost too quietly.

"Okay. Have you seen Agent Dill?"

"Rather slightly."

"Oh, and where is he at?"

"On his way to the hospital, Bill."

"Why is he on the way to the hospital?"

"I found him all shot up in the parking garage a few minutes ago. He asked me to not let Agent Stallingsworth get away with the killings," replied Michael, almost ready to cry.

"Oh my God! Stallingsworth shot him up?!"

"Yes, and he is on the way to the hospital. Here's the arrest warrant for Stallingsworth," said Michael, as he threw down the paperwork on top of the desk.

The blood soaked warrant landed with a splat on the desktop. Bill looked down at it and nearly vomited. As Bill looked up again, Michael was turning around and getting ready to leave. Bill mustered up enough courage to keep the vomit down as he tried to think of something to say to Michael. It was Michael that broke the silence.

"The ball's in your court, sir," said Michael as he walked out the double-doors.

Michael went home that afternoon after having stopped by the airfield to practice flying. This four hours of flying time gave Michael a chance to sort through all the feelings that he was experiencing at that time. As Michael drove home, he was mentally uptight, and trying to relax only made the feelings stronger.

He parked his car and walked up to his apartment. He opened the door and walked into his apartment. After closing the door behind himself and locking both locks on the front door, he cried silently to himself. Never in his life had he experienced what he had in just the past few weeks. Looking around the apartment, he found a flashing light on his phone.

Casually, he walked over to the phone and picked up the receiver. He dialed the access code number for the phone to retrieve messages. As the mechanical voice went over the number of messages and their times, he noticed one was from just about two hours ago. He put the receiver up to his ear and pressed the number seven key to listen to his messages. The first message was from Stallingsworth.

"Hello, Michael. I'm sorry that I didn't finish off your team, but I kind of ran out of time, as you would say. Don't bother tracing this phone call, because it won't do you any good. I'm a free man and you're going to be dead soon. Tallyho!" the message stopped.

"I'll get you if it's the last thing I ever do on the face of this planet," said Michael, loudly.

The next message was unexpected; it was from Bill.

"Michael, this is Bill. I tried to reach you by cell phone, but you must have turned it off. I understand how you feel. Trust me. I was there when my teachers all went bad. Listen, I need you to check in with me tomorrow morning, right away; goodbye," was all Bill had to say.

Michael went to bed late that night. He set his gun on the nightstand and took a shower. After the shower, he said good night to the picture that was on the dresser and turned off the light. Michael didn't get much sleep that night, for he kept having the same dream over and over again. The dream was of him being laughed at by Stallingsworth as Stallingsworth tortured him until he died.

Stallingsworth was laughing hysterically at Michael as Michael tried to save his own life. Michael woke up, sat up in bed and noticed that even though it was cool in his apartment, the sheets on his bed were soaked in sweat. He rolled over and looked at the clock, it was 0500 hours.

He stepped out of bed and went into the kitchen. He fixed himself some breakfast and then went back to the bedroom. Once he had retrieved his weapon, he carried it out onto the balcony. He sat down into one of the two lawn chairs out there. As he looked eastward, Michael saw the rising sun and it brought him a strange sense of peace.

The peace, though, was short lived for soon everyone around him was starting out his or her day. TVs and radios were being turned on and breakfasts were being made. Michael finally went inside, locked the sliding glass door behind him and got dressed for the day.

At a few minutes past 0800 hours, Michael called Bill's office. Agent Everett answered the phone and transferred the call to Bill. Bill almost ripped the receiver off the cradle when he found out who it was on the phone.

"Michael, I'm glad that you called as I instructed you. Can you come in here today, say, at about 1300 hours?" asked Bill nicely.

"Sure, see you then," said Michael, as he hung up the phone.

Bill hung up his receiver and sat back in his office chair. Bill's secretary buzzed him. Bill reached over and grabbed the receiver.

"Yes?" asked Bill.

"Madam Secretary of State Lillian Winks is on line 1 for you."

"Thank you, Miss Everett," replied Bill, pushing the flashing line on his phone.

"Yes, Bill, what can I do for you?" she asked, even though she already knew what the request was going to be.

"I need your authorization to activate procedure 070," said Bill.

"Procedure 070 is to be used when we either have, or suspect we have, a renegade SPOT agent. I believe that procedure requires that the suspected renegade SPOT agent be either tried for his or her crime or crimes and then executed, am I right?"

"Yes, ma'am, you're quite right. I have probable cause that SPOT

Agent Stallingsworth is a renegade and is responsible for the deaths of all my SPOT agents, except two," replied Bill.

"Why did you wait as long as you did before you called me?"

"I wasn't sure if it really was a renegade SPOT agent until just recently."

"What evidence do you have to support this theory of yours?"

"Agent Stallingsworth lied to Agent Dill during an investigation about a weapon that was supposedly reported as stolen, lost or damaged. Agent Stallingsworth was known not to like the new person I chose to run the SPOT detail here in Denver; namely one Michael Pigeon. He was positively identified by Agent Dill as the person who shot him up in the parking garage."

"That is enough evidence. I will draft up the paperwork outlining the specific details to attempt to capture this renegade SPOT agent. Please be ready to receive my fax on your secure fax line by 1200 hours Mountain Standard Time today."

"Thank you, ma'am and have a nice day," said Bill hanging up the phone.

At a little before 1200 hours Mountain Standard Time, the secure fax machine came to life. The fax machine spit out 20 sheets of paper and then stopped making noise. Bill walked over to the fax machine and looked into the catch tray. There, on the last page of the fax was the signature he was looking for; the Secretary of State Lillian Winks.

He turned the fax over and immediately had Agent Everett make a copy for him. When she returned with the copy, she handed Bill a small stack of paperwork with her signature on the last page. Bill looked at the paperwork and then up at her.

"Are you sure you want to retire?" asked Bill.

"Yes, I am sure. I want to stay alive, considering what has happened to the rest of the team," she replied.

"So noted. I will complete your personnel action forms by the end of the week."

"Thank you, sir."

As she walked out the door, Michael was coming into the outer office. She waited until he had entered the office before closing the double-doors behind him. She took the liberty of locking the doors this time instead of Michael. As Michael walked towards Bill's desk, Bill stood up to shake hands with him.

"Michael, glad you came to see me today," Bill started off saying.

"What's going on now?" asked Michael, almost without feeling in his voice.

"I have received the official orders that you are hereby designated by the Secretary of State Lillian Winks to hunt down and bring to justice one renegade SPOT Agent Wayne Stallingsworth. Here is your authorization paperwork. Please keep it with you at all times," said Bill, handing Michael the fax.

Michael took it and briefly looked over it before setting it down on the desktop. He looked up at Bill for some sort of help, but he found none. Only the Cobalt blue eyes stared back at him. Michael picked up the paperwork and walked out the door. As he walked passed Bill's secretary's desk, he looked at Agent Everett.

"I could use a hand on this mission, Agent Everett," said Michael.

"I can't help you, Michael. You're on your own," she replied.

"What do you mean, 'I'm on my own?'"

"I handed my resignation in about half an hour ago to Bill. I want to live, not die."

"I understand. However, could you do me one favor?"

"What's that?"

"Get me in touch with a judge that can sign another arrest warrant since the other one met with a terrible demise."

"I can do that."

Michael continued walking down the hallway towards the elevators. Once he was at the elevators, he walked out into the parking garage and drove home. He realized that, for the first time, he was really alone on this mission. However, he decided that he would bring Agent Stallingsworth to justice at any cost.

Michael called Bill to find out the current status of Agent Dill. Bill informed Michael that Agent Dill was tough and had survived those gunshot wounds. Bill went on to say that Dill would probably recover from the wounds, but would probably be medically retired from the SPOT Agent Program.

Michael pressed Bill to find out the exact condition Dill was in at the hospital. Bill finally told Michael that the official report was critical but stable. Dill was in the intensive care unit of Denver General Hospital. Bill had taken the precaution of placing guards around Dill in case Stallingsworth tried to finish the job.

Michael hung up the phone feeling much better than he had the whole day since finding Dill in the parking garage. Michael sat down at the kitchen table and opened the envelope up. His mission was simple; hunt down and bring the renegade Stallingsworth to justice at all costs. For Michael, that seemed simple enough. In fact, for Michael, he fancied himself a worldwide bounty hunter.

CHAPTER 8

▼

The next morning was starting out worse for Michael than ever. A sudden snowstorm had rolled through the area during the night and left its mark on everything. He decided today he would take the Light Rail System into work since his car was covered with snow.

As he walked out the door with his pass in hand for the Light Rail System, he wondered how hard it would be to track Stallingsworth down. He walked into work and went straight up to Bill's office to see what was going on with Agent Dill. He walked into the outer office and former SPOT Agent Everett looked up at him.

"Good morning, Michael. Bill wants to see you," she said.

"Thank you. Have you heard any word on Agent Dill's recovery?" he asked.

"No, he is still in intensive care, listed as critical, but his condition this morning was upgraded."

"Upgraded to what?"

"Critical but stable condition. If he can progress to serious, but stable condition, then he can leave the intensive care unit."

"Sounds good. Well, I guess I had better see what Bill wants."

Michael walked into Bill's office. Bill was already on the phone and was hanging the phone up when Michael walked into the office. Michael shut the double-doors to the office and sat down in the chair opposite Bill's left side. Bill looked at Michael and smiled.

"Good morning, Michael. I just got off the phone with the hospital. Agent Dill should be able to leave the hospital in a few months."

"Sounds good. I gather, by the paperwork that you gave me yesterday, that I'm some sort of an international bounty hunter?" inquired Michael.

"Yes, however there are a few restrictions that have been placed on your duties."

"What kind of restrictions?"

"You can't go get him if he is in a foreign country that doesn't have an extradition treaty agreement with the United States."

"Okay."

"Also, even if the foreign country has an extradition treaty with the U.S., they may not release him to you if he might possibly face the death penalty."

"He should die for his crimes as far as I'm concerned."

"I know how you feel about this, Michael. But, you're the only SPOT agent that I have left. You're also the last person that Stallingsworth would suspect of trying to arrest him."

"Well, I'll make sure that the handcuffs and ankle shackles are well oiled."

"Trust me, I've been in your shoes before many years ago. It was harder in those days to track someone down."

"Why was it harder to track someone down?"

"Most of us didn't know how to operate a computer. We had to rely on others to do it for us. Of course, they weren't always loyal to some of us and sometimes we were sent on wild goose chases."

"So you want me to track him down and then go get him, right?"

"Essentially, yes. You're the best agent we've had in the SPOT program in some 20 years or more."

"Thanks for the compliment."

"You'll get him, I have every confidence in your abilities. The only thing that I ask is, please inform me before leaving the country so that I can alert our SPOT details in the area that you're going to be there."

"I think that's a good idea alerting the other SPOT units in an area that I'm operating for safety measures."

"Just keep me informed as to what your progress is on this case. You have many resources available to you, use them."

"Okay, anything else?"

"No. Have a good day."

Michael walked out the door and back out into the outer office. As he walked passed former SPOT Agent Everett's desk, she looked up at him. She smiled and handed him the arrest warrant, still stained with Agent Dill's blood and now wrapped up in a plastic bag.

"Michael, in reference to what you asked me to do yesterday. You have an appointment with The Honorable Judge Melanie Cisneros."

"What time?" replied Michael, taking the plastic bag from her and putting it into his left suit jacket pocket.

"1100 hours today. Her chambers are located in the federal courthouse."

"Thank you, Agent Everett."

"You're entirely welcome, Michael. I will do my best to help you as much as I can. I hope that you're not holding some sort of grudge against me for retiring."

"No, not at all. In fact, after I thought about it last night, you're right, maybe after this assignment, I might turn in my papers as well."

"No you won't. I know you too well. There's a certain thrill in being a SPOT agent for you."

"Well, thanks for the help anyways."

"Don't be late."

Michael looked at his watch. It was reading 1015 hours. He walked down the hallway towards the elevators. When he arrived at the elevators, he pushed the call button and stepped into the elevator when it arrived. He waited for the doors to close before pushing the button for the lobby. When the elevator doors opened again, he found the lobby full of people. He proceeded across the lobby to the main entrance doors. He opened the doors and stepped out into the cold morning.

He took in a couple of deep breaths before walking towards the federal courthouse. Thankfully, although it was cold and snow was everywhere, he didn't have far to walk. He had walked about 12 blocks and saw the newly redesigned and recently finished federal courthouse. He entered the courthouse and passed through security.

Thankfully, Michael had left his weapon at home today or else he would have had to do a few other things while proceeding through the security checkpoint. He handed the security officer his identification and the security officer entered him into the logbook. As the security officer handed back his identification, he then saw the red markings on the identification.

"Are you armed, sir?" asked the security officer.

"No, I left my weapon at home today."

"Would you submit to a search so that I can verify this statement?"

"Sure, not a problem."

The security officer escorted Michael through the other security checkpoint and into a small room. The room had no windows and only the one door. The security officer had Michael take off his jacket and turn around. After the security officer performed a "pat-down" on him for hidden weapons, he gave Michael back his jacket. As they were leaving the room, the security officer turned to Michael.

"Thank you for submitting to the search of your person. The Honorable Judge Melanie Cisneros' chambers are on the fourth floor."

"I am not familiar with this building. How do I get there?" asked Michael.

"Take the elevators to the fourth floor. When you step out of the elevators, turn to your right and open the large double wooden doors. Her chambers are number 404 and have a nice day."

"I will."

Michael walked over to the elevators and pushed the call button. There were a lot of people here in the lobby and Michael wondered if he could ever get an elevator. For Michael, he had to wait a few extra minutes before he was able to get an elevator. He saw that someone had already pushed the button marked for the fourth floor.

In a few minutes, Michael stepped out of the elevator along with a few other people. He turned to his right and saw the large, wooden double doors that the security officer had spoken about earlier. He opened the doors and entered a long hallway. He was able to find a secretary sitting outside a set of four doors. Casually he approached where she was sitting at and smiled as she looked up.

"Can I help you, sir?" she asked pleasantly.

"Yes, I have an appointment with The Honorable Judge Melanie Cisneros," replied Michael.

"Let me see. Your name is?" she asked, looking over her appointments list.

"Michael Pigeon."

"Yes, sir. I will let The Honorable Judge Cisneros know that you are here," she said, picking up the phone and pointing to a group of chairs that was behind Michael.

Michael turned around and saw the chairs that she indicated. He walked over to the chairs and sat down in one of them. The first thing he noticed was how uncomfortable the chairs were. Michael looked around the room he was inside. There were two doors to his left and two doors to his right. There were plaques on all of the doors.

The plaques were located to the left of each door, as you would face them. Michael didn't have to wait long before the second door to his left opened up and a young-looking woman exited. She looked at the secretary and then across the room at Michael. She walked over to him and extended her hand.

"Michael Pigeon, I'm Judge Melanie Cisneros. I believe we have an appointment today," she said.

"Yes, Your Honor we do have an appointment," replied Michael, almost choking on his words.

The judge was nothing that Michael had expected her to be. He was expecting someone in their late 50's or early 60's. He also imagined her with silver or gray hair and frail looking. This judge was anything but that and he couldn't help staring at her.

"Is there something wrong, sir?" asked Judge Cisneros.

"No, not really. I was expecting someone older, that's all," said Michael, sheepishly.

"I get that kind of reaction all the time. I'm 35 years old in case you're wondering. Please come into my chambers," she said, indicating with her right index finger pointed towards the open door.

Michael followed her into her chambers. As Michael walked into her chambers and found the one and only seat in her chambers, he sat down and looked around. She shut the door and Michael heard her lock the deadbolt lock on the door. She came around from his right and sat down in the high backed leather chair behind her desk.

"So, Mr. Pigeon, what can I do for you today?" she asked.

"I need an arrest warrant reissued, Your Honor," he said.

"Did the other arrest expire or something?" she asked.

"The other arrest warrant, Your Honor, had an accident before it could be served."

"An accident?" she inquired.

"Yes, Your Honor," replied Michael, pulling out the plastic bag. He handed the plastic bag to Her Honor for review.

She took the plastic bag and looked at the arrest warrant. It was covered in blood and almost unreadable. She then turned it over several times to see who had been the original judge to sign the warrant. She found the signature and immediately recognized the signature.

"Is that blood on this arrest warrant?" she asked, nervously.

"Yes, Your Honor, it is blood," replied Michael.

"Is the law enforcement person who tried to serve this warrant dead?"

"No, Your Honor, he is at the hospital listed in critical, but stable condition."

"Very well," she replied.

She reached into her desk and withdrew another arrest warrant. She turned around to her computer that was sitting directly behind her and turned it on. She then inserted the new arrest warrant into the printer and started clicking away with the mouse.

In a few minutes, the new arrest warrant was printed up, based off of the information contained in the original arrest warrant that was already in the system. She pulled out a pen from her right shirt pocket and signed the warrant. She then handed the warrant to Michael.

"This arrest warrant is valid for the next 15 days. If you cannot serve the warrant on the subject named on the front of this warrant, you must get the warrant reissued again. Do you understand this instruction?" she said.

"Yes, Your Honor, I do."

"Very well," she said, after completing the signature.

She handed Michael the new arrest warrant. She then took the old one, plastic bag and all, from Michael. Michael looked at her strangely as to why she took the other arrest warrant from him. She placed the plastic bag containing the blood stained arrest warrant into a brown paper sack with red and white diagonal stripes on the outside.

"What are you going to do with the old warrant?" asked Michael.

"In accordance with Rule 41, as amended, this warrant must be destroyed. No duplicate warrants are allowed in the system," she replied.

"Okay, I understand now. Thank you, Your Honor, for your time today."

"Not a problem. Have a good day."

Michael left her chambers with the new arrest warrant. Michael decided to stop and have lunch before going back to Bill's office. He stopped at a submarine sandwich shop. He arrived back at the State Department building and went to Bill's office to check-in. He also checked on the condition of Agent Dill. There was no change in his condition.

As Michael entered the outer office again, he smiled at Everett. She smiled back and then continued to type up the dictation that Bill had left for her. Michael walked into Bill's office and shut the double doors behind him. He then took a seat in the chair that was to Bill's right as he sat facing out. Bill was on the phone once again. Michael waited until Bill was finished before looking at him.

"Michael, good to see you. Did you get the arrest warrant reissued?" asked Bill.

"Yes, I did. Is there some place where I can start a file folder on this mission?"

"Sure, you can use my office. That far filing cabinet is not in use and I have plenty of file folders for you to use."

"Great. Let me get to work, okay?"

"Sure. Did you have lunch yet?"

"Yes, I did, before I returned to the office."

"Well, I haven't had lunch yet. The office is yours until I get back," said Bill, as he left the office in a hurry.

Michael went over to the filing cabinet and opened up the top drawer. There were hundreds of hanging file folders in the drawer. Michael pulled out a few of them and set them down on Bill's desktop. He then looked around on Bill's desktop and found the pen and pencil holder.

Soon, he located a large black marker and started marking the file folders. After he had finished marking several file folders, he put the arrest warrant into one of them and closed the drawer. At that time, Bill had returned from having lunch and smiled at Michael.

"Bill, is there any way of locking up this filing cabinet?" asked Michael.

"Sure there is, here's the key," replied Bill, handing Michael an odd looking key.

"Thanks, Bill. I'm going to start by looking over some of Agent Stallingsworth's missions. There might be something in there that might give me a clue as to his whereabouts."

"Sounds like a good starting point. Michael, I have all the confidence in the world in you that you will find him and bring him to justice," said Bill confidently to Michael.

"I'm glad that you have confidence in me. I just hope that I can live up to those expectations," said Michael.

Michael left the office and headed down into the records vault. The records vault technician gave Michael a printout of the operations that Stallingsworth had ever been involved with since he became a SPOT agent 17 years ago. Michael saw that the list was very large and some of the case files were labeled as "RESTRICTED" which meant that Michael could not access them without a security clearance of the next level up. Michael started off alphabetically going from A-Z.

He discovered that Agent Stallingsworth was a man who didn't always go by the book. During some of his missions that Michael read through, he was anything but a rulebook player. He often did things on some missions that ranged from simple and dangerous to over the edge outrageous.

Although he was reprimanded for the actions each time, Michael noticed that Lillian Winks had always kept him from being expelled from the SPOT agent program on several occasions. She signed letters of commendation that seemed to override the letters of reprimand.

Michael pored over many case files over the coming days and weeks. To Michael's frustration, he could not find a connection to any of the missions and where Stallingsworth might be hiding. Time soon took on a new meaning for Michael. Everyday was the same for him, he would start out reviewing files and then he would go home at the end of the day with many pages of notes.

He was trying to find some common denominator in tracking

Stallingsworth down. It had occurred to Michael that he didn't have a picture of Agent Stallingsworth. As Bill entered the office one day, Michael approached Bill.

"Bill, would it be possible to obtain a picture of Agent Stallingsworth? I think it might help my investigation," said Michael.

"Sure. In fact, let me print you up his picture right now."

Bill went over to his computer and powered it up. He then used the mouse and clicked a few icons and soon, on the color printer that was sitting next to Michael, a color picture of Agent Stallingsworth printed out. Michael grabbed it and put it into one of the file folders in the filing cabinet. He then shut the drawer and locked it up. He looked down at this watch and saw that it was time to go to his hand-to-hand combat lesson downstairs in the building's gym. As he was leaving, Bill stopped him.

"Michael, Agent Dill was upgraded today. Although he is still in intensive care, his condition is now listed as serious, instead of critical," said Bill.

"That's wonderful news and thank you, Bill."

Michael went downstairs to the building's gym and worked out with the hand-to-hand combat instructor. After the workout, he returned to the office and started his usual afternoon compilations of his notes. Nothing in any of the case files that he had looked at, except for the ones that he couldn't look at because they were restricted, added up.

However, he did notice that Agent Stallingsworth had many powerful friends from the Secretary of State, to the Assistant Secretary of State to members of Congress and the Senate both. Michael knew that finding Agent Stallingsworth and bringing him to justice would be an almost impossible task. He was willing to put forth the effort because Michael felt he owed it to the other SPOT agents that Stallingsworth had killed to give them some sense of closure.

Michael went home that night and found another message from Agent Stallingsworth on his phone. Again, Stallingsworth informed Michael that he was well hidden and that he couldn't be found. Michael deleted the message and said to himself, "We will see about that." Michael took a shower and went to bed.

CHAPTER 9

▼

Time for Michael was going by very quickly. Weeks soon turned into months and months into the first year. The good news was that Agent Dill was expected to make a full recovery in a few more months. He was walking short distances already and he was talking better now that he didn't have a breathing tube shoved down his throat.

One bright, spring morning, Michael came into work and received a shock when he walked into Bill's office. There, standing on crutches and carrying a small oxygen bottle with him in a backpack, was Agent Dill. He turned to face Michael.

"Thought you might need some help with Stallingsworth," said Dill.

"I sure do. What's your current status?" asked Michael.

"Medically retired by personnel standards because I cannot do my job anymore. However, there's nothing to prevent me from assisting you with Stallingsworth's case."

"I think I've reached the end of the road with this one, Agent Dill," said Michael.

"It's just Dill, or Henry, if you prefer. I'm medically retired, remember?" said Henry.

"Sorry, I forgot."

"That's okay. How much evidence do you have as to where he might be?"

"Almost none."

"Bill, if it's alright with you, I would like to assist Agent Pigeon with his case."

"I don't have any objections unless Michael has some."

"I don't have any objections. In fact, I could sure use the help."

"Michael, I'm having a retirement party in Miami next week. Why don't you come there and relax?" said Henry.

"That sounds like a great idea, Michael," replied Bill.

"Okay, I'll see you in Miami next week, Henry," replied Michael.

"Goodbye, Bill and Michael."

Henry left the office and Michael opened up the filing cabinet. He pulled out several file folders of notes and started going over them. As the day progressed, Michael stopped only for lunch and then to call it a day. He arrived back at his apartment a little after 1800 hours. Once he was inside and the doors were locked, he fixed himself some dinner and then stretched out on his couch.

Around 2145 hours, he stepped into the shower and then went to bed. However, he didn't sleep well at all; a recurring dream of Agent Stallingsworth's laughing face kept waking him up periodically. When the alarm clock went off, Michael didn't really want to get out of bed. He did anyways and went into work.

Michael was pouring himself a cup of coffee, putting cream and sugar into it. He walked over to the filing cabinet, unlocked it and pulled open the second drawer. Since he had almost filled the top drawer up with various notes, he had expanded to the second drawer. The second drawer was where he kept his other notes.

Notes that he had taken on all of Stallingsworth's cases. He began going over the notes once again when Bill walked into his office. He looked over at Michael who looked back up. Bill walked over to Michael and handed him a package. Michael took it into his left hand and then opened it up. Inside were round trip airfare tickets to Miami, Florida for Henry's retirement party. Michael put the airline tickets into his right shirt pocket and went back to poring over his notes.

By the end of the day, Michael had found nothing conclusive. The only irregularities in Stallingsworth's operations were the expenses and equipment damaged or destroyed during a mission. With precious else to go on, Michael called it a day once again and went home. When he arrived at home, he found another message in his voicemail from Stallingsworth.

This time, however, he could hear something faintly in the background. Saving the message, he thought, would help him in his case somehow. Michael started packing his clothes for the trip to Miami. During the plane trip, Michael finally had a chance to sort things out.

The retirement party was great. There were lots of other current and former SPOT agents there. Some of them knew Michael, although he had not met them personally. They all thought he would be the best SPOT agent to track down Stallingsworth and bring him to justice.

As the party was winding down, Henry waved at Michael from across the room. He motioned for Michael to follow him to the basement. Michael followed Henry down into the basement and Henry shut the basement door and locked it.

"So, Michael, having any luck at all?" asked Henry.

"No and I wish he would quit calling me," replied Michael, rather irritably.

"He's been calling you?"

"Yes, every few months or so I come home to find a voicemail message on my phone. I listen to the messages and then delete them. Except for this last message."

"What was different with this message versus the others?"

"This message was different because I could hear something in the background."

"What was it that you could hear?"

"It sounded like surf in the background, along with someone or something playing music and singing horribly off key."

"That is very significant, Michael. You don't let too many things get passed you do you?"

"No, Henry, I try not to let anything get passed me."

"Any phone numbers show up on your Caller-ID®?"

"No, he said he was using something that would prevent his phone number from showing up. Those annoying beeps in the middle of the message are starting to get on my nerves."

"Annoying beeps? Michael, those beeps are from an unregistered phone scrambler. Those beeps, unknown to him, are traceable."

Michael stood there for just a moment looking at Henry. Michael then looked down at the floor and then up at Henry once again. Henry looked back at Michael.

"Here's what I think you should do, Michael. Get a seizure warrant for your voicemail and get the phone company service technicians to put that voicemail onto a compact disc. Take that disc to the crime laboratory personnel and have them feed the voicemail message into the computer. Have the computer analyze the sounds for comparison," said Henry.

"Okay, I'll do that when I get back. Right now, I'm tired and I think I'm going to go back to my hotel room and go to bed. My flight leaves early tomorrow. Where's Bill?"

"He came here earlier and left on the late night flight," replied Henry, knowing that it was a lie. Bill wasn't going to be at the party; Henry just needed an excuse to get Michael to Miami so that they could talk.

Michael left Miami early the next morning. Before 1000 hours, Mountain Standard Time, he landed in Denver, Colorado. He went to the office and filled out an affidavit asking for seizure of his own voicemail message from Stallingsworth. He walked outside the office and looked at Everett.

"Is there something I can do for you, Michael?" she asked.

"Yes, I need to obtain a seizure warrant."

"Okay, let me call the courthouse and see when that can be done, okay?"

"I'm going to lunch, just let me know."

"I will."

Michael had returned from lunch to discover that Everett had secured the seizure warrant. Michael's next step was to go to his telephone company and serve the warrant. He served the warrant on the telephone company shortly after 1330 hours that day. The technicians were able to retrieve his voicemail that he had saved and put the voicemail onto a compact disc.

Michael returned to the office building and went into the basement. The crime laboratory technician took one look at the "CHAIN OF CUSTODY" form attached to the compact disc and called his supervisor. The supervisor took the disc from Michael and looked at him.

"What do you want me to do with this, Mr. Pigeon?" asked the supervisor.

"There are some sounds on the voicemail that I think are surf and someone singing terribly off key. I need both of them analyzed," replied Michael.

"Yes, sir. I can't tell you how long it will take. Where can I get in contact with you when the results come through?"

"Bill Yancy's office, upstairs on the eighth floor."

"Yes, sir."

Michael went back up to Bill's office and Bill looked at him as he walked in and smiled. Bill was drinking his cup of afternoon tea when Michael opened up the filing cabinet and rummaged around inside of it for a little bit. Michael then carefully closed the filing cabinet back up and locked it. As he was leaving, Bill spoke to him.

"Michael, any luck on the case yet?" asked Bill, nonchalantly.

"Yes, I'm awaiting the results of the laboratory tests that I asked to be run on my voicemail message from Stallingsworth."

"He's been in contact with you?"

"Yes, periodically I will get a call from him taunting me to come and find him. It's the annoying beeps from his unregistered phone scrambler that are getting on my nerves."

"He has an unregistered phone scrambler?"

"Yes, but no one seems to know what to do about it."

"I do, Michael. First of all, an unregistered phone scrambler will keep sending out those registration tones until they are properly answered. Then it will be quiet," replied Bill, smiling.

Michael thoroughly listened to what Bill had said. He replayed it a couple of times in his head before he smiled at Bill. Michael even went as far as to nod his head up and down. Bill had left Michael a hint and Michael had actually picked up on the hint. Michael left Bill's office and turned around to face Everett again.

"Miss Everett, could you possibly get me a phone scrambler registration device?" asked Michael.

"I think something can be done about that issue; good night, Michael."

Michael went home and stayed there all the next day. He phoned Bill to tell him he was checking out some bank account information and some credit card information. However, Michael was headed for the airfield and where the chartered jets depart from. He parked his car and walked into the chartered jet office. He withdrew the picture Bill had printed out of Stallingsworth. As Michael approached the check-in desk, a man looked up from the desktop.

"Can I help you, sir?" he said.

"Yes. Do you recognize this man?" asked Michael, thrusting the picture of Stallingsworth in front of the man. The man looked at the picture and then looked up at Michael.

"Yes, I do remember him. Kind of a strange fellow, a last minute authorized passenger on State Department Flight 1757."

"What name did he give you?"

"Wayne Stallingsworth and he had several suitcases with him at the time."

"Who authorized him to jump aboard Flight 1757?"

"Let me see, Lillian Winks was the name attached to his flight voucher."

"Can I get a copy of Flight 1757's flight plan?"

"Sorry, since September 11, 2001, that information is restricted. You do understand that, right?"

"Yes, I do. Thank you for your help."

Michael left the airfield feeling much better. He stopped by the office and ran into Bill. Bill looked up as Michael came into the office.

"I wasn't expecting to see you here in the office. Has something come up?" asked Bill.

"Yes, Stallingsworth was added as a last minute passenger by none other than Lillian Winks, the day of the search of his house. He was long gone before Agent Dill got there. However, an old man at the airfield recognized Stallingsworth's face by the picture that you printed up of him. That same old man identified him as a last minute passenger aboard State Department Flight 1757."

"Do you know where the jet went?"

"No. I guess I will be seeing my favorite judge on Monday morning to get another seizure warrant for Flight 1757's flight plan."

"You're doing great, Michael. Don't rush things now that they seem to be turning your direction."

"I won't. I guess I will spend the weekend writing up an affidavit for the seizure warrant."

"Sounds good to me. However, I have some paperwork for you," said Bill, handing Michael a seizure warrant for his apartment. Michael took the paperwork and then looked back at Bill.

"What did you take?" asked Michael, all flustered.

"Nothing. We did that as a formality so that we could install the phone scrambler registration device to your phone."

"Oh, I get it, so the next time Stallingsworth calls, I'll know where he's calling from, right?"

"Exactly. The device is in place. When he makes his next call to you, your Caller-ID® should register the phone number."

"I appreciate all the help you're giving me, Bill."

"Oh, by the way, see the crime lab personnel in the basement, they have some information for you."

"I will; goodnight."

Michael left Bill's office and headed for the basement. He walked down the hallway towards the elevators and pushed the call button. The elevator car arrived and he stepped into it. As the doors closed, he pushed the button marked for the basement, level three. When the doors opened again, he walked down the short hallway to the crime laboratory.

The door was shut, so he looked around the doorframe. He located a sign that read, "IF THE DOOR IS CLOSED, PLEASE RING BELL ONLY ONCE AND SOMEONE WILL COME RIGHT OUT TO ASSIST YOU. THANK YOU." Michael located the buzzer on the left side of the doorframe as he faced it. A few seconds later, the supervisor that Michael had met earlier showed up and let Michael inside the laboratory.

The supervisor showed Michael down a short hallway that ended at a large, wooden door. The man reached into his right front pants pocket and pulled out a key card. He put the key card into the key card reader and then pushed a series of numbers into the numeric keypad attached to the card reader. The door slowly opened and Michael stepped into a whole different world.

The room was full of computers and all sorts of peripherals. The man took Michael to the back part of the room. They entered a smaller room and Michael sat down with the supervisor. The supervisor put on a pair of glasses and started reading the report that had printed out from the computer earlier during the day.

"The sounds in the background weren't easy for the computer to positively identify. Right now, the computer is only giving us 80% odds that the conclusion it has arrived at is accurate," the man started off saying to Michael.

"80% is better than nothing," replied Michael.

"The computer is 80% sure that the sound in the background is indeed surf. Specifically, the type of surf that you might find along the shores of the Pacific Ocean."

"How can the computer be that certain?"

"The computer has accessed and compared over 2,275,000 different surf sounds. It has determined, like I said, to 80% accuracy that the sound is from somewhere in the South Pacific Ocean."

"Okay, that leaves about 60,000 square miles of ocean to search, then," said Michael, sarcastically.

"Very funny. The other sounds on the compact disc were the unregistered phone scrambler registration request tones. The person you thought was singing off key was in fact a South Pacific Islander singing a tribal tune of some kind."

"Can the computer tell you where at in the South Pacific that the tune came from?"

"Yes. I asked it for an analysis and the computer narrowed it down to Hawaii, Guam, the Philippines and a small chain of islands near the Sumatra Trench near Indonesia."

"Thank you, you've been a great help today," replied Michael, as he took the printout and went home.

At home, Michael found two voicemails. One from Bill asking if Michael needed any time off and how much he would need and the other was from Henry. He called to see how things were going. Michael decided that it probably wasn't too late to be calling the Eastern Standard Time Zone.

"Good evening, Michael how are you doing?" said Henry in a cheerful voice.

"Great and I would like to tell you thank you for all your help."

"Any time. What about the voicemail, any luck there?"

"Some, Bill has installed a phone scrambler registration device to my phone line so that if Stallingsworth calls, I can get him."

"Sounds good, Michael. Now, you're entering a most dangerous time for you. Please slow down and be careful."

"You know, Bill said the same thing."

"He's a good man. However, if Stallingsworth calls, you have to keep him on the line for at least 45 full seconds for an accurate location."

"Oh, Bill didn't tell me anything about that."

"Probably slipped his mind. What's that beeping noise?"

"I have call waiting. Hang on, let me find out who it is."

"Okay, I'll be waiting for you."

Michael hung up the phone and answered the other call. The call was from Stallingsworth. He was talking like he was drunk, slurring his words and then he started laughing as he hung up the phone. Michael took the phone away from his ear and checked the length of the call; 40 seconds. "Not long enough," thought Michael. He then returned to Henry.

"Who was it?" asked Henry.

"Our friend. I wish he would quit calling me."

"How long was he on the line?"

"Only 40 seconds, but now his phone scrambler is registered."

"That's good. Call Bill and have him print out the number. I think Stallingsworth has just made his biggest mistake."

"Goodbye," said Michael, hanging up the phone.

Michael called Bill. Bill told Michael to stay by his phone and that Bill would call him back. A few minutes later, Bill called him back with bad news; Stallingsworth hadn't been on the line long enough for a full trace. However, Stallingsworth's phone scrambler was now registered.

Michael took a shower and went to bed. This time around, he slept better than he had in some time. No more nightmares with Agent Stallingsworth laughing at him and tormenting his nights. Michael was getting closer to finally having some sense of closure to this mission.

CHAPTER 10

▼

Michael could feel his blood beginning to boil. Even though Stallingsworth had not been on the phone long enough for an accurate tracing, his unregistered phone scrambler was now registered. Michael hoped that he would call him again and this time, stay on the line long enough for an accurate trace. The phone company technicians said they might be able to squeeze a few extra seconds out of him being on the line.

They reprogrammed the phone's ringer to ring an extra two seconds and delay two seconds in between rings. Michael was concerned that Stallingsworth might notice this extra time. The technicians assured Michael that Stallingsworth wouldn't notice the extra time. This might give Michael what he was waiting for; Stallingsworth's number.

He went into work as usual the next morning and found out from Everett that the seizure warrant had been signed. Michael walked down to the courthouse and picked the warrant up and drove out to the airfield. He presented the warrant to the man behind the counter. The man logged into his computer and then printed out the flight itinerary, giving it to Michael. Michael took the itinerary back to the office and started going over the plane's flight.

According to the flight itinerary, the plane made 11 stops. Out of those stops, various equipment, cargo and personnel were exchanged. Michael looked over the stops and found that there were at least four of them in the South Pacific area. Michael was pouring himself a cup of coffee when Bill walked into the office. Bill looked up at Michael and then down at the stack of papers on his desk.

"Doing some research or is all this paperwork a clue?" asked Bill.

"A very large clue, Bill. Sorry, I'll clean off the desktop," replied Michael, who put his cup of coffee down on the coffee table and cleaned off the papers from Bill's desktop.

Bill smiled and sat down at his desk. He looked over in Michael's direction after reading through his morning messages. One of the messages was from the crime laboratory stating that Stallingsworth wasn't on the phone long enough for an accurate trace. However, the lab was able to obtain the serial number of the unregistered phone scrambler.

They suggested to Bill that the serial number be checked to see who had purchased the item. They also went on to say that they did have a partial phone number. They said they would turn this critical information over to Michael whenever he wanted to come down to the laboratory. Michael was busy poring over the flight plans when Bill walked over to where he was sitting.

"Michael, when you get a chance, go downstairs and talk to the crime lab personnel," said Bill.

"Sure, I could use a break right now."

Michael put the flight plans into the filing cabinet and locked them up before leaving Bill's office. He walked down the hallway and pushed the call button for the elevator. In a few minutes, Michael was walking down the hallway towards the crime laboratory. He found the door open and walked right into the office area. A female looked up and smiled at him.

"Good morning, Mr. Pigeon. I'll let Dave know you're here," she said, picking up the phone.

Michael didn't have long to wait. Dave, one of many supervisors, came out a side door almost immediately. Dave took Michael down the hallway to the forensics part of the crime laboratory. He waited until Michael was inside the room before shutting the door.

"Michael, I have some good news and some bad news for you; which one first?" asked Dave.

"Bad news first, please," said Michael.

"I wasn't able to get the entire phone number that Stallingsworth was calling from, however, I was able to get the country code and the city code though," said Dave, handing Michael a computer printout.

"That's very good, now how about the good news," asked Michael.

"We traced the serial number of the phone scrambler to a piece of equipment that had been issued to Stallingsworth during *Operation Flim-Flam.* He reported the equipment on a Form 1464 as lost or damaged during the operation."

"Thank you, Dave, you have been a great help to me."

"Anytime, Michael anytime."

Michael returned to Bill's office and logged into the computer terminal. He then called the phone company directly after not finding the location of the partial phone number on an Internet search. He reached over and picked up the phone receiver that was next to him and pushed a button for one of the many outside lines. He dialed the number for international information and had to wait several minutes before anyone answered the phone.

"Thank you for calling International Information, this is Lydia, how can I help you today?" she asked, pleasantly.

"Yes, Lydia, can you tell me something about a phone number?"

"Yes, sir, I certainly can. What number do you have?"

"62-6-179. Unfortunately, the rest of the number is not visible on my Caller-ID®."

"One moment, sir."

Michael could hear the sound of her fingers roaring over the keyboard. She placed Michael on hold for a few more minutes before returning. She picked up her phone line and talked to Michael.

"The number in question starting with the country code of 62 is identified as Indonesia. The next number, 6, indicates that the call came from a small island chain called the Sunda Islands. The last three numbers that you gave me, 179, tells me that this is the city code where the call originated. Is there anything else I can help you with today, sir?"

"No, you have been a great help; goodbye," said Michael, hanging up the phone.

It was after lunch that Michael finally put all the pieces of the puzzle together. He wrote all the information down in chronological order and then started pacing around the office until he came up with the only conclusion that fit the facts that he had uncovered during his investigation.

The Secretary of State, the Assistant Secretary of State and the Deputy Secretary of State, among others, were doing lots of illegal things, such as approving murderers to leave the country, among other things. Michael stopped pacing as Bill opened the door to his office.

"Good afternoon, Michael. Anything new to report?" asked Bill.

"Yes, that phone call came from the Sunda Islands."

"The Sunda Islands you say, let me look and see if they have an extradition treaty with the U.S.," said Bill.

Bill walked over to a small, two-drawer filing cabinet. The front of the drawers were both locked with a combination lock. Bill worked the combination lock and the top drawer opened. He reached into the drawer and pulled out a large book.

He shut the cabinet drawer and spun the dial a couple of times. He then walked over to his desk, set the book down on his desktop and opened it up to the index page. He then thumbed through the book until he was almost in the middle of it and then looked up at Michael.

"I'm sorry, Michael, the Sunda Island government does not have an Extradition Treaty with the U.S.," said Bill, closing up the book and putting it back up into the filing cabinet.

"So, I guess that's the end of the trail then, isn't it?" asked Michael.

"No. We have other options and I will be happy to explore them with you if you want," replied Bill.

"Yes, I would like that very much."

Bill spent the remainder of the afternoon, which soon turned into the early evening, on the phone with various people in New York City at the United Nations building. He was on the phone with people on the West Coast as well. Bill had just finished off the last phone call of the evening. He looked over and found Michael snoozing on the couch. Bill looked down and stared at the massive amount of information that Michael had amassed.

Bill started reading some of the conclusions that Michael had drawn based off of the evidence Michael had accumulated during the more than 14 months of investigative work. Michael soon felt Bill trying to wake him up. Michael woke up to find a phone receiver in his face.

"Who is it, Bill?" asked Michael, as he sat up to take the call.

"Henry," replied Bill, as he handed Michael the phone and then Bill left his office.

"Hello, Henry, how is it going?" asked Michael.

"Very well, thank you. I just got off the phone with Bill. He says you think more people are involved than what we think?"

"Yes, sadly enough there are a lot of other people."

"Do you have enough evidence to obtain arrest warrants on those people?"

"Not complete enough evidence. All I have are some signatures and authorizations on some paperwork."

"Tell me more," said Henry.

"Well, I found out that Stallingsworth falsified at least two Form 1464's for various pieces of equipment. The funny thing is, both of those forms were signed off for by various State Department personnel."

"Let me guess, Lillian Winks."

"One of several."

"Who are the other ones?"

"The Assistant Secretary of State and the Deputy Secretary of State had their hands in this mess as well. Lillian's signature on the flight plan of State Department Flight 1757 allowed Stallingsworth to leave the country,"

"She is slick. Michael, be very careful, watch out for her and her cronies. They may have anticipated that you might be able to figure out what was going on. They may have set up booby traps for you, if you know what I mean."

"I know what you mean. I know where Stallingsworth is."

"Where?"

"A small island chain in the South Pacific called the Sunda Islands."

"Let me guess, no extradition treaty with the U.S.?"

"That's right. I'm ready to give it up, Henry, the frustration isn't worth the price if Stallingsworth goes free."

"I know how you feel. Trust me, I've been there and done that. You did say the Sunda Islands, right?"

"Yes."

"Michael, I might be able to help you there. For now, I want you to sit back and let me handle this issue."

"Okay. You will call me when you have something?"

"Yes."

Michael hung up the phone as Bill was walking back into the office. Michael handed Bill the receiver and Bill hung the phone back up into the cradle. Bill then looked down at Michael.

"Is everything all right?" asked Bill.

"Yes, for now."

"Michael, I hope you won't become too upset with me, but I made a copy of your conclusions and gave them to a friend of mine at the FBI field office here."

"Your friend probably laughed in your face, didn't he?"

"No. In fact, some of the evidence you obtained actually helped his case out against the Secretary of State and others within her department."

"You mean to tell me that this is a big thing?"

"Yes, in fact, it might go as deep as 30 to 40 people. Right now, my friend is trying to get the arrest warrants on the Secretary of State and her friends so that they can be brought in for interrogation."

"I hope my conclusions weren't wrong."

"I don't think they are. Besides, you have been trying to track down Stallingsworth for almost 16 months now. Why don't you just go home and wait for my phone call."

"Okay, besides, I'm a little tired."

As Michael was leaving the building, he stopped by the armory and picked up his .357 magnum revolver and took it home with him. He opened the door up to his apartment and found a message on his phone. He sat down and accessed his voicemail and expected it to be from Stallingsworth. The voicemail was from Henry. Henry wanted Michael to call him immediately. Michael called Henry late that night on the Eastern Coast of the United States.

"Michael, is that you?" asked Henry.

"Yes, it is. Now, what is going on?" asked Michael in return.

"I called in an old favor. Do you have a piece of paper and a pen to write with?"

"Yes, just a moment," replied Michael, as he fumbled around through the desktop for a message pad and a pen. He located one and started writing down the information that Henry gave him.

"You have an appointment with the Sunda Island Ambassador on Friday, the 29th of this month, in New York City. His name is Ambassador Fodor Achem. You are to meet him and his interpreter at the front entrance to the United Nations building at around 0800 hours."

"0800 hours on Friday the 29th of this month, I wrote that down."

"Michael, I want you to keep these things in mind while talking with the ambassador."

"What's that?"

"The man represents a country that is harboring a cold blooded killer. His country is also strapped for money right now. He is also a military man. Did you get all of this?"

"Yes, I did."

"Don't blow this chance to get Stallingsworth. Tact and diplomacy may get you what you want. However, don't rule out other means to getting the goal."

"I understand, Henry and good night."

Michael hung up the phone and looked at the calendar. It was going to be two weeks before Michael was going to be able to meet this Ambassador Achem. Michael decided that he would be prepared with a full statement to give to Ambassador Achem. He then started packing his best clothes and his identification to allow him to carry a firearm. He went to bed that night feeling a little better about himself and the whole situation in general. He set his alarm clock to go off and then went to sleep.

The next morning, Michael went into work and put in a time-off request. He placed the request on Bill's desk and then left the office. Neither Bill nor his secretary had seen Michael come in because Michael had waited to put the request on Bill's desk while they were both in various staff meetings. Bill came back to his office, saw the time-off request and indicated he had approved it by his signature. Bill then placed the paperwork into the OUT going basket to be handled by personnel. Michael returned to the office a few hours later.

"Good morning, Michael. I received your time-off request and approved it for the dates indicated. Do you have anything planned?" asked Bill trying to gather information.

"Yes, I'm going to New York City to see an Ambassador Achem at the United Nations."

"Please be nice to the ambassador."

"I will. Well, my work here today is almost finished," said Michael, grabbing the now expired arrest warrant and taking it with him.

Michael went to the federal courthouse and waited to see The Honorable Judge Melanie Cisneros. She came out of her courtroom and saw Michael standing there. She didn't say anything to him, but she did motion him into her chambers. After the door was shut and locked, she sat down at her desk.

"Well, Mr. Pigeon, what can I do for you?" she asked.

"I need this expired arrest warrant reissued, Your Honor," said Michael, almost choking on his words.

"Let me see the warrant, please."

Michael handed her the expired warrant. She looked it over to make sure that he wasn't trying to make her sign another warrant for someone else. She reviewed the warrant and then turned around to her computer. She pulled up the warrant number on her computer and inserted blank arrest warrant paperwork into her printer. She hit the print key and the arrest warrant was reissued for another 15 days. She signed the warrant and handed it over to Michael.

"Thank you, Your Honor," said Michael as he stood up to leave the room.

"Michael, you work for the State Department, don't you?"

"Yes, Your Honor I do work for the State Department, why?"

"I heard there might be some changes in the main office in Washington D.C. soon. Good luck," she said.

"Thank you, Your Honor."

Michael walked out the door and returned to his apartment. He finished packing and purchased airfare using his own personal credit card. Michael didn't want to use the government issued credit card for the purchases. Finally, the day had arrived for Michael to leave. He took a taxi out to Denver International Airport and after clearing through security he boarded his plane. A few hours later, he was landing at John

F. Kennedy International Airport. After deplaning, he went down to the baggage claim area and retrieved his luggage.

Soon, Michael was outside waving down a taxi to take him to a hotel that would be close to the United Nations building. The taxi driver asked him if money was an issue. Michael replied no, money was not an issue. The taxi driver took Michael to a very nice hotel that was only a few blocks from the UN building. Michael checked in and set his alarm clock early so that he could have breakfast before meeting with the ambassador. The alarm clock went off the next morning and Michael prepared for the meeting.

After breakfast, he put on his suit and locked up his gun in the safe that was in the hotel room. He then rode down in the elevator to the lobby level and walked out the front doors into the rising sun. He walked about only seven blocks before he saw the entranceway to the UN building.

The entranceway was ornately decorated with the flags of the nations that were represented there at the UN. Michael walked up the entranceway and stepped into the bustling lobby of the UN. Looking down at the floor in the lobby, he saw the symbol of the UN. A few minutes after he arrived, a small Asian looking person approached him.

"Are you Michael Pigeon?" the person asked with a slight accent.

"Yes, I am," replied Michael.

"Please come with me, the ambassador is expecting you."

Michael followed the man into one of several elevators and they rode up to the ninth floor. When they exited the elevator, the man turned to face Michael.

"You will have only one hour with the ambassador. Please keep it short."

"I will."

They walked through the outer office and into the inner office. The ambassador turned around in his chair to face him. They shook hands and Michael handed his written statement to the interpreter. The interpreter then read the statement to the ambassador who seemed to Michael to be very interested in what was being said. After the interpreter had finished the reading, the ambassador turned to face Michael and spoke.

"I understand your position, Michael Pigeon, but my country has no extradition treaty with the United States of America at this time.

However, I do understand that you are a special friend of Henry Dill," said the ambassador through the interpreter.

"Yes, Henry Dill is my friend, Mr. Ambassador," said Michael.

"How is he doing?" asked the interpreter.

"Not well. He was medically retired from the SPOT service a few months ago," replied Michael.

"How did this happen?"

"The man that I seek in your country is the one who shot him up and then fled to your country via a chartered jet flight."

"We would like to help, but we cannot at this time."

"I understand, Mr. Ambassador, that you were once a military man; even killed people, perhaps?"

"Yes, so what is it of your concern?"

"The man who sought refuge in your country killed 14 people."

"I have killed people before, Mr. Pigeon."

"Even you aren't as cold-blooded as the man I seek."

"I would like to help, but the U.S. seems to be stingy on money matters."

"I see. Well, Mr. Ambassador, I might be willing to make it worth your while if you will help me by signing the extradition treaty today."

"My country is very poor and this man you seek is providing a good income to lots of my people. If I do sign this treaty, will the sentence on the crimes he committed in your country be punishable by death?"

"No. A good jury or a good attorney might only give him life without parole."

"I cannot sign this treaty. I am sorry. Have a good day, sir."

"Let me say this one last thing. One of those people that he killed was a seven-month-old baby in his crib with a .45 caliber pistol. The ball is in your court, Mr. Ambassador and have a good day. I will leave you my phone number if you should decide to change your mind."

"Very well."

Michael left and went back to his hotel room. He was frustrated and angry at a judicial system that seemed to lack any sense of moral right. As he sat on the edge of his bed after dinner, the phone rang. He picked it up and recognized the interpreter's voice.

"Mr. Pigeon, I have thought a lot about what you said earlier this morning. I have signed the extradition treaty as of an hour ago. I have scratched your back, now you have to scratch mine."

"I hear you, Mr. Ambassador. I will deliver one hundred thousand dollars in cash tomorrow morning."

"That is very good. I look forward to seeing you tomorrow morning at 0900 hours."

"Thank you, sir."

"Even I am not cold-blooded enough to kill an infant."

"I didn't think you were."

The next morning, Michael went to one of the larger banks in New York City and withdrew the cash from his personal credit card. The money was placed into a briefcase. This time he was carrying his gun when he went to see the ambassador. The interpreter escorted him up to the ninth floor and when the doors were closed to the inner office, Michael opened up the briefcase and dumped the stacks of $100 bills on the ambassador's desk.

"As I understand the laws in your country, you have an arrest warrant for this man?" asked the interpreter.

"Yes, right here," replied Michael, dropping the arrest warrant down on the desktop.

"It will be served on this man. He will be extradited back to the U.S. to stand trial in 24 hours. Is that good enough?"

"Yes, sir. Have a good day."

Once Michael had left the UN building, he felt much more relaxed than he ever had been. He wasn't going to find out until a few weeks later that the Secretary of State and at least 45 other government officials within her Cabinet were arrested and charged with various charges.

Michael had the privilege of escorting Stallingsworth to federal court for his arraignment. He filed his final report to include a copy of the receipt for one hundred thousand dollars. Michael asked that foreign aid to the Sunda Islands be implemented immediately.

Michael realized that, more than once, he could have blown the whole case and Stallingsworth would have walked away free. Somewhere within him, some Higher Power decided that patience was to be taught. Michael decided to finish off the vacation in Hawaii.